D1197530

NORTH FROM IDAHO

The minute Anderson landed at the remote Idaho rail station, he knew he'd find trouble. Some people out there wanted him dead. They'd started with a bushwhacking at the station house, and when that didn't work they kept right on trying. Just like he knew they would. When he woke up in a funeral parlour after a saloon gunfight, Anderson thought it couldn't get much worse, but pretty soon he realized he was wrong. From Idaho the trail led north into the Canadian wilderness, where a bunch of outlaw killers waited . . .

JEFF SADLER

NORTH FROM IDAHO

Complete and Unabridged

LINFORD
Leicester

First published in Great Britain in 2004 by
Robert Hale Limited
London

First Linford Edition
published 2005
by arrangement with
Robert Hale Limited
London

British Library CIP Data

Sadler, Jeff, *1943* –
    North from Idaho.—Large print ed.—
Linford western library
1. Western stories
2. Large type books
I. Title
823.9'14 [F]

ISBN 1–84617–016–8

Published by
F. A. Thorpe (Publishing)
Anstey, Leicestershire

Set by Words & Graphics Ltd.
Anstey, Leicestershire
Printed and bound in Great Britain by
T. J. International Ltd., Padstow, Cornwall

This book is printed on acid-free paper

1

He stepped down from the train and into the biting cold, knowing death waited for him.

In front of him the timber-framed station building loomed, its roof draped with a hanging shelf of snow that dripped finger-length icicles down over the porch. Anderson grimaced as the raw chill struck his face, hefted his gear and the heavy Texas saddle more securely on to his shoulder as he made towards it, the Winchester carbine held right-handed at the trail.

They were here already, he could tell.

Underfoot the ground was frozen hard, ice-slick and treacherous to his booted tread. Anderson edged across it as best he could, flinching as the bitter cold turned his ear-rims to frozen fire and reached to chill his flesh through the thick plaid coat. His left leg had

1

begun to throb with a dull, half-remembered pain as cold woke the old arrow-wound to plague him. That he could have done without, he figured.

Scanning the stretch around him, he found nothing suspicious in plain sight. Platform and station building both looked to be deserted, and only a handful of passengers straggled off the Pacific locomotive that stood whistling and belching smoke from its funnel, coming to rest at this stop in the middle of nowhere. Anderson spared a glance for the red-faced whiskey-drummer, the young schoolma'am and the overripe female with two bawling kids in tow as they struggled past him for the shelter of the station house.

No sign here for most to read, but he knew better. Anderson had lived close to death for longer than he cared to remember, and over the years he'd learned to trust his instincts. They were here, all right, and now they were waiting to gun him down.

Far side of the station house, away to

the right, lay a man-high pile of old timber baulks, disused railroad ties from the look of them. Beyond them he made out the shapes of a couple of timber wagons, ice gleaming pale on their sides. Anderson notched them, stored them in his mind in readiness. Good enough for a bushwhacking, he thought.

He felt the hair spring up on the back of his neck, an instant before a shifting movement behind the woodpile con-firmed his reaction. Anderson shrugged off saddle and war bag, brought up the carbine to snap off a quick shot in the direction of the move. He was already diving forward as his finger pressed the trigger and flame lashed from around those timber sleepers. The flat cracking sound of the Winchester drowned to a heavier, deafening boom that battered his ears and threw back echoes from the walls of the station house, the air suddenly thick with flying buckshot.

Hitting hard, icy ground, Anderson rolled and came up for a second try.

This time, though, he didn't waste his time on the *hombre* behind the timber pile. Sonofabitch had tried for him with both barrels, and right now he'd be reloading.

He had the carbine lined on the window of the station house in the moment the second bushwhacker showed, rearing up above the sill with the weapon filling his hands. Another shotgun, just like he'd figured. He triggered again, the .45–70 slug smashing into the sill to throw up a spray of wood slivers that sent the *hombre* ducking with both hands to his face. Anderson didn't stick around to watch, rolling again to drive up on to his feet. His kick drove the door back, slamming on its hinges to hit the wall, and he lunged in along the narrow corridor ahead, crouching low as he reached left-handed to haul the .45 single action Army from leather. Behind him he could hear a woman screaming, and the scared voice of the whiskey-drummer calling out for help. He only hoped that none of them had been hit.

4

The door to the station office lay off to his left. Anderson dived by it as the shotgun roared from inside, buckshot ripping the panels to flinders that struck and clattered off the wall above him. Anderson listened to the ugly noise of the buckshot spray as it thudded into timber, his dark face grim and unforgiving. Lucky for him the feller was aiming for an upright target, and he'd stayed low again. Way he saw it, the bastards had taken their best chance, and missed. Now he figured it was his turn.

He was back around, both weapons levelled on the ragged, gaping hole in the door as the would-be killer showed. Anderson caught a glimpse of a burly, thickset *hombre* in store clothes, his broad features clenched tight as he hurried to lift the sawn-down shotgun. The dark man beat him to it, touching trigger on the Colt the instant his target filled the gap, Winchester braced on his right hip as the carbine fired a split second after. Both heavy slugs smashed into the bushwhacker before he could fire, hitting with murderous force to hurl him backwards from sight. The shotgun slipped from his hands, clattering to the floor near to its intended target. This time, it didn't go off.

A spasm of pain shot through his left leg, and Anderson winced, struggling to his feet. Trust the goddamned wound to play him up at a time like this, he thought. He set down the Winchester on the floor of the corridor, holstered the Colt to pick up the fallen shotgun. Eyeing the weapon, he nodded in approval. Twelve-gauge Greener, loaded and ready. Anderson's lean face broke to a grim, pitiless smile. He'd used one of these before now, and knew how deadly they could be.

The second *hombre* wouldn't have moved yet. To hit the station house, he'd have to break cover and risk being gunned down in the open. Better to stay put, and let Anderson come to him. That was just what Anderson aimed to do, but maybe not the way the killer had it planned.

He didn't go on through the back door of the station house. To his right lay another door, and Anderson used the shotgun barrel to edge it slowly back. Stepping inside, he found himself in what must be the passenger waiting-room. No passengers around, or shotgun-toting killers either. At the far end he made out an empty window, its tarpaper blind removed. Anderson shivered as a draught of freezing air blew inside. He moved quickly across the room, wincing as pain stabbed through his left leg, and flattened himself against the wall, peering out through the corner of the window. It was a while before he caught sight of the other gunhawk, but Anderson wasn't in any hurry. He could afford to wait.

A couple of long, slow minutes passed before he glimpsed the flicker of movement beyond the woodpile. The killer edged back from the mound of sleepers, moving for cover behind the railway wagons. Right now, he was well out of shotgun range, but he wasn't looking towards the window. He had his eye on the rear of the station house, waiting for Anderson to come out of that back door and round the corner of the building into reach of a killing shot. Looked like he was due for a surprise.

A slat-backed wooden bench stood close to the window. He clambered on to it, hauling the shotgun after him. Anderson grabbed the sill, swung a leg to slide awkwardly through the narrow gap. He reached back to grab the shotgun by its barrel, dragging it through behind him as he slithered down the icy wall to hit the ground. Kind of dangerous toting the weapon that way, but he guessed that was how it had to be.

The *hombre* heard the noise as Anderson came out through the window, but by the time he whipped around to aim he was already too late. Anderson went to the ground, holding the Greener two-handed as he headed for the woodpile at a desperately hurried crawl on elbows and knees. He was almost at the woodpile when the gunhawk made his play, easing out around the nearest wagon to loose off both barrels again. Thrown by Anderson's unexpected move, he hurried his shot. Buckshot sliced the air in a fanshaped spray overhead, and the dark man dropped flat to the dirt, face close to ice-coated ground as metal fragments spattered to earth some yards behind him. He was up and into cover then, pushed up close to the woodpile with his own weapon lifted, but found himself with nothing to shoot at. The killer was back behind the wagon, somewhere out of sight.

Anderson stole a quick glance around the nearest timber baulk, and found no sign. For a while he stayed put, waiting, then backed up warily, edging his way round the far side of his new-found shelter. Going low on hands and knees, he headed for the far corner of the pile. The move brought him out closer to the wagons, and for the first time he saw the *hombre* who was so set on putting him underground. Right now the feller was half-hidden between two of the wagons, shielded by the nearest from a direct shot, but Anderson saw enough to know that he was tall and long-limbed, dressed in a flat-crowned, broad-brimmed hat and the kind of black Prince Albert coat he'd seen some gamblers wear. What counted most, though, was the twin-barrelled shotgun held out ahead of him as he scanned the other side of the woodpile, and waited for Anderson to show.

Anderson frowned, feeling the cold bite him through the knees of his pants. From here, he didn't have anything like a clean shot, and if the gunhawk had any sense Anderson knew he wasn't about to move on the woodpile just yet. Only one thing for it. He had to go in himself, and smoke the jasper out.

He left the shelter of the woodpile, holding the shotgun forward as he struck away towards a point above and behind the wagons. Almost as he made the move the *hombre* heard him, whirling around for the shot. Anderson dived away as the shattering boom of the shotgun came after him. This time the volley was a way closer, too close for his liking. Anderson yelled out as a stray slug lashed the back of his neck, felt the jolting impact of other pellets that struck and lodged in his shoulder and hip. The main force of the charge missed him by a couple of feet, ploughing into the ground and sending clods and ice shards flying across his back. The *hombre* was into cover by the time he rolled over and brought the Greener level on the wagons beyond. Anderson slithered in closer, flinching at the pain of the slugs in his six-foot frame. Right now the shotgun felt like a hundredweight of lead, and it took a real effort to hold it steady.

He made it to the nearest wagon and huddled tight against the nearside wheel, barely feeling the touch of frozen metal through his thick plaid coat. Safe enough for now, but it left the gunman out of sight, shielded by the wagon wall. Almost as he settled, Anderson heard the clip of booted feet on icy ground, and read what it meant. The bushwhacker was heading around the far side of the wagon, aiming to hit him from behind. No chance of a body shot now, but there were other ways.

Fighting the pain of the wounds that throbbed through his body, Anderson slid the shotgun out ahead of him, lying flat to bring the wooden stock to his shoulder. Beneath the wagon, he saw the black-clad legs of the bushwhacker, the hand-tooled boots that stepped towards the corner of the wagon. The dark man lined up ahead, braced himself as he pressed the trigger.

The recoil pounded his shoulder, and he bit back a cry of pain. Then the booming roar of the shotgun swallowed everything, punishing his eardrums as the wagon-bed trapped the noise and hurled it back at him. As the echoes died, he heard the high screaming of the stricken man on the far side of the wagon. Anderson coughed, choking in a billowing cloud of gunsmoke. He slid out from underneath, struggling to keep a tight hold on the Greener, and hauled himself up against the wagon-bed. Peering around the side, he saw the long-framed jasper floundering on all fours, leaving a bloody trail behind him as he tried to reach his fallen shotgun.

'Just leave it be, feller!' Anderson told him.

The *hombre* didn't answer. Instead he grabbed the weapon, twisting painfully to a sitting position as he swung it upwards for a one-handed shot. Anderson braced the Greener with his free hand, and triggered off the second barrel. The Double-O charge blasted the gunhawk in the chest, flung him backwards and down like a lopped pine. This time he stayed put.

The last thundering echoes died away, the evening suddenly loud with the clamour of voices. Anderson let the shotgun fall, leaned for a moment on the wagon-frame before moving to the fallen man. The *hombre* rolled over to the prod of his foot, limp as an empty sack. Anderson looked down into a pale, thin-featured face whose hard eyes stared back at him, lips pulled back from the teeth in a final snarl of thwarted fury and pain. A face he'd never seen before in his life. Below it, he guessed he didn't need to look too hard. The shotgun blast had torn the *hombre*'s chest to a mess of ugly red holes, and there wasn't too much left of his legs. Anderson swallowed on a foul, brassy taste. A mite less luck, and he'd have been lying there, he thought.

He covered the dead man's face with the flat-crowned hat and started back for the station house. Pain clawed at him from old and fresh wounds alike, and he hobbled like an oldster, aware all at once of the blood that seeped through his shirt and coat. Suddenly he felt way colder than before, so tired the weariness went down to his bones. By the time he neared the station house, the passengers were running to meet him.

'You all right, young feller?' The whiskey-drummer blocked his path, staring at him anxiously. On the train, his face had looked ruddy enough to catch fire all by itself, and Anderson guessed he'd already tried a few free samples of his wares, but now his features were the colour of flour, like he'd just seen a ghost.

'I'll live,' the dark man told him. His glance went past the drummer to where the schoolmistress and the plump matron stood watching him. The two kids hung on to their mother's skirts, their faces turned from him. 'None of you folks hurt, I hope?'

'We're all fine, mister,' the young schoolteacher answered. Like the others, she was still kind of pale, and scared too, he figured, but no way was she about to show it. 'It's just a shock, that's all.'

She took a closer look at him, and Anderson saw her eyes go wider as they glimpsed the blood that leaked from the ragged hole in his sleeve.

'You're hurt!' At once her voice expressed concern as she reached towards him. 'Your neck's cut, too. Those wounds need tending.'

'In a while, maybe.' Anderson waved her away, stumbled a little as he turned. 'Right now you folks better stay here. I have to check out the station house.'

'But we have to get you to a doctor!' Her voice came after him, angry and impatient. Like she wasn't used to taking no for an answer. Maybe all schoolma'ams were that way, he thought.

He made for the station house, limping heavily as pain flared in his hip, swore under his breath as his weight came down on the left leg. Anderson eased the Colt free before he reached the entrance. The door still hung back on its hinges, and he stepped into the corridor warily, edging along the wall towards the splintered door of the office.

The first gunman lay where he had

fallen, sprawling on his back where the gunshots had thrown him. Anderson met the fixed, shocked stare of the eyes, scanning the broad sun-tanned face of another stranger. He holstered the .45 Army, breath leaving him in a weary sigh as it smoked in the cold.

From across the room came moans and muffled cries for help. Anderson limped around the scarred desk with its scattered papers, saw the two trussed-up figures who writhed helpless on the floor. Stationmaster and porter, both tied and gagged like turkeys for Thanksgiving. Reaching awkwardly with his unwounded left hand, he drew his hunting-knife from its sheath, and hurried to cut them loose. Both men yelled like they'd been stuck as the ropes came off, but that was a good sign. He hauled off the gags, and waited for them to get back to breathing again.

'Thanks, mister.' The stationmaster rubbed at his punished wrists, light from the kerosene lamp putting a glistening sheen on his balding crown.

He reached to grasp Anderson's hand, pumping it fiercely in a two-handed grip. 'Much obliged to you, young feller. If you hadn't turned up, Jane an' me might just've smothered to death in here.'

'Goes for me too, mister.' The porter was thin and scrawny as a starving crow, but now his hollow-cheeked face cracked into a grin. He grabbed the tall man's hand as the stationmaster let it go, and put it through a second shaking. 'Jake Hanson's the name, and mighty glad to know you.'

'My pleasure, gents.' Anderson hoped he didn't sound as tired as he felt. 'Joshua Rankin, just come through from Coeur d'Alene.'

'You're surely welcome, Mr Rankin.' The stationmaster beamed, flexing his wrists more easily. 'Homer Canfield, I'm stationmaster here at Riggott.' Glancing beyond Anderson and the dead gunman towards the doorway, his face grew a wary expression. 'You see the other one?'

Anderson answered him with a grim, silent nod.

'You know either of 'em?' he asked, and both men shook their heads.

'Never seen 'em before,' Canfield told him. 'They showed up maybe a couple of hours back, rode in here from the north. First thing me an' Jake knew, we was lookin' into a pair of shotguns. Wasn't too much we could do about it.'

'You just said they rode in,' Anderson reminded him. 'They leave their horses here?'

'Tethered out back, I guess. We heard 'em rein in behind the station house.' Canfield sounded puzzled. 'Why'd you want to know, Mr Rankin?'

'I'm headed north from here myself,' Anderson told him. 'Way I hear it, there ain't no trains up from Riggott, an' I left my regular mount back at Coeur d'Alene. If you gents got no objection, I aim to help myself.'

He turned in the narrow doorway, pain from the hip wound slowing him as he hoisted his fallen carbine.

Anderson made it to the corridor, and through the back door of the station house. In the yard out back the tethered horses stood steaming in the cold, shifting hoofs against the frozen dirt. The dark man looked them over, and nodded approvingly. Both were good animals, but he favoured the tall bay gelding that stood nearest to him.

Beyond the yard and its rail fence came Riggott, a sprawl of squat log-walled shacks that showed darker on the gathering dusk. The buildings seemed to huddle closer against the cold, roofs and walls glistening with ice. Anderson felt that chill cut through him, breath smoking into the thin air as his gaze swept on beyond the town. Out into the distance north Idaho's panhandle stretched away in a broken wave of gullies and forested slopes, dense stands of pine and spruce climbing up for the foothills of the mountains. Further off, the jagged peaks of the Cabinets cut the skyline in a knife-edged silhouette, their summits black and stark against the fiery sunset. And beyond them, more forests and more mountains, all the way north to the border. The way he was headed.

He left the wall of the station house, starting towards the horses. Pain bit viciously in his hip and shoulder, and Anderson grimaced, putting a hand to the wall to steady himself.

'Mr Rankin!' That was the schoolma'am again, and she sounded sterner than ever. 'Mr Rankin — I believe that is your name — come back here this minute!'

He tried to ignore her, pushing from the wall, and the left leg gave way under him. Anderson swore feebly, slithering down on his haunches. Suddenly he found it was too much of an effort for him to get up again. Turning his head, he saw the young woman standing in the open doorway, studying him severely over her wire-framed eyeglasses. Behind her the red-faced whiskey-drummer jostled Canfield and Hanson in the corridor, wheezing for breath as he clutched Anderson's saddle and gear in both his hands.

'Got to get from here, ma'am,' the dark man told her. He tried to struggle up, lost the carbine as he fell back.

'You are going nowhere, Mr Rankin,' the schoolma'am informed him. Behind the spectacles her pale features were fierce and determined. 'Those gunshot wounds need attention, and well you know it. I see I shall have to attend to this myself.' Rounding on the group, she barked out her commands. 'You, put that saddle down and help me get him inside. Meanwhile I'd be obliged if you two gentlemen would boil me some water. We shall require a substantial quantity.'

Watching them scurry to obey, Anderson guessed that any other time he'd have found it kind of funny. Right now, though, he just felt weak and sick and weary to his bones. He didn't fight the young woman or the drummer when they lifted him and helped him back along the corridor and into the office.

'Don't worry, Mr Rankin,' the schoolma'am was telling him as she helped him into the nearest chair. 'My mother was a nurse with the Army in the War between the States, and I made it my business to learn from her.'

'Sure do appreciate this, ma'am,' the tall man said. Right now, he hoped he sounded better than he felt.

This job had already turned out tougher than he figured, and Anderson had the feeling that he'd yet to see the worst of it.

2

But for the dog, he'd have been dead meat.

Snow hit them suddenly, a blinding flurry of thick pelting flakes that came streaming out of nowhere and through the timber to hammer man and horse alike. Guiding the tall appaloosa forward, head ducked against the blizzard as he fought to stay clear of the frozen stretches in the shadow of the trees, Sharrock almost blundered into the trap. Lucky for him, Abe stayed smart and was first to catch the scent as it blew towards them.

Sharrock saw the huge, brindled dog freeze for an instant, ears up and alert as the long muzzle lifted, and read the warning. He swung the horse off the trail and down a long slope to his right, pitching himself sideways out of the saddle the moment they cleared the crest. He slapped at the appaloosa's flank as he dropped clear, sending the critter on at a run for the foot of the slope, the grey blur of the dog going past him as the first shots spat from the timber. Sharrock hit frozen dirt, the old Sharps clutched tight in his gloved hand, and went rolling downhill with the breath knocked out of him. Above on the rim he heard the whiplash cracking of other carbines, and the ugly sound of bullets that ripped through pine boughs and splattered bark from their trunks. Sound of an ambush that hadn't worked first time, and was no longer a surprise.

Down at the bottom of the slope he struck and stayed put, hefting the Sharps as his keen eyes scoured the pines for a target. The horse turned around, coming back to him, and Sharrock reached out to tap the animal's shoulder with the carbine barrel.

'Down, feller!' Sharrock said. He went back to ground, sliding in behind a clump of rocks and thorny brush as the big horse rolled over and lay still. Almost as he landed, the brindled dog shoved in beside him, snarling and baring its teeth as the hackles came up along its neck. Sharrock grinned tightly, laid his hand gently on the massive head.

'Stay put, Abe,' he told the animal.

Flame stabbed from away on the left, the slug whining like a hornet through the thickening snowfall. He heard it crack into ice somewhere behind him, paid it no mind. Sharrock fired for the gunflash, levered fast to put another shot close to the side. He broke cover the moment he fired, heading right and up the slope at a run, making for the thickets and boulders higher up, that now grew a heavy covering of snow.

Licks of tawny orange flame slashed the white torrent of the snowfall, and with them the vicious whine of bullets cutting air apart. Sharrock dived for the shelter of a boulder clump, hearing the bitter crack of carbine fire follow the shots like a belated echo. Two more bushwhackers could be heard over to his right, both of them hurrying their shots now they realized that their first wild volley hadn't put him away. Their efforts fell short, throwing ice and snowy slush up along the rim. Sharrock notched their gunflashes, whipped up like lightning to trigger over the flat top of the boulder, aiming ahead and to one side. He caught the blundering crash of bodies through the timber as both men sought cover further back, snarled as the *hombre* on the left tried for him again. This time the slug hit rock and ricocheted, wailing like a tormented soul as it ploughed into brush behind him.

Sharrock got off a rapid shot in answer, struck right and on for a stand of pines on the crest. Behind him came a harsh, deep-throated growl, and Abe went hurtling past him at a lope. One of the bushwhackers sent a stray shot singing after him, but the hound was way too fast, already out of sight as the trigger was pressed. Crouching among the pine roots, checking the Sharps for reloads, Sharrock began to smile faintly. He figured Abe already had the scent, and knew what the dog had in mind. It was a trick the two of them had pulled before. No reason it shouldn't work now.

He stayed down, waiting until the feller on the left lost patience enough to edge around the pine trunk that hid him, sliding the carbine barrel out in front. Sharrock was a touch too quick with his shot, swore as the bullet ploughed into the pine bole and missed the man behind it. His face stung by flying hunks of pine, the bushwhacker yelped and gave back deeper into cover, Sharrock heading closer around the trees on the ridge as fresh shots came from the timber on his right. This time they were further off, and their efforts spat harmlessly short, thudding into the black trunks of the pines with their hanging freight of snow.

'Hey, Charlie!' The sound came as a

bull-like bellow, echoing through the trees. Listening, he recognized it right away for Tevis's voice.

'Goddammit, where is he, the sonofabitch?'

'Over yonder!' The answer was high and pained, the *hombre* on the left still slapping pine flecks from his eyes. 'Leastways, he was a minute back!'

Darting to fresh cover in the trees, Sharrock's smile grew a cruel edge. Tevis and Fairchild, huh? Had to be Magruder's bunch, just like he'd figured. Sharrock had come up against better in his time, and run out ahead. Right now, he was counting on it staying that way. Crouching low in the shadow of a pine trunk, half-blinded by pelting snowflakes, he clutched the carbine and waited. Wouldn't be long now, he thought.

The cold metal of the Sharps had begun to chill him through his leather gauntlets when other sounds broke from further back in the timber. High, piercing squeals of terrified horses, and after them the ferocious snarling of the dog as Abe launched his attack. Hearing them, Sharrock nodded, fingering the trigger-guard of the carbine. The hound had had their scent from the first. Wouldn't have taken him no time to find them.

He started forward, going at a run between the dark boles of the trees. Away to the left he heard the crash and splinter of twigs underfoot as the first bushwhacker went back in a hurry for the screaming horses, scared of being cut off from his pals. In front he heard Tevis yelling frantically above the noise of the scared animals and Abe's snarling.

'Goddammit to hell! Get back, both of you! That black son's runnin' off our hosses!'

Sharrock ducked into the snowfall, running through deepening drifts towards the sound. Further off, the terrified squealing grew louder, and the three horses broke to sight, charging through the timber with their trail-ropes hanging loose, Abe growling and barking as he loped wolf-like after them. Watching them run, Sharrock chuckled through the flakes that spattered his face. The bushwhackers had left the critters ground-hitched, figuring they wouldn't be disturbed. Sometimes the dumb bastards never learned.

Branches shook to his right, and two men broke cover, yelling and flailing their arms as they floundered through the snowdrifts in pursuit of the horses. Sharrock recognized the massive, hulking frame of Bull Tevis, in company with some ferret-faced little *hombre* he hadn't set eyes on before. Half-way into the trees, the pair of them halted, the smaller man hoisting his carbine for a shot at the running dog. Sharrock triggered in the same moment, saw the bushwhacker flinch away with a yelp of pain. A second try from the Sharps plugged the hat from Tevis's head, and the two of them ducked back into the timber, stumbling after the horses. By now, he figured, Charlie Fairchild would be hurrying to join them.

Sharrock put gloved fingers to his lips, and gave a whistle that cut keenly through the other sounds. Soon as he heard it, Abe doubled back and came bounding back to where his master stood waiting.

'Done a fine job there, Abe,' Sharrock told him. He stroked a hand over the thick, bristling fur of the hound that growled and brushed up against him, its massive head level with his chest. 'Between us, we fixed 'em good, I reckon.'

He stood, paying no mind to the heavy snowfall that swirled around them, plastering man and dog from head to foot with a coating of thick white flakes. His body felt like it had been hammered to hell and back, and he guessed he'd be sporting some bruises come morning, but nothing appeared to be badly damaged, and that was what counted. Sharrock turned, whistling for the horse, and the appaloosa regained its feet, stepping carefully up the slope to join him on the crest. Sharrock took hold of the dropping rein, and climbed into the saddle, stowing the carbine in its leather scabbard.

The bushwhackers would be no trouble for now, he knew. It was likely to be a while before those horses tired enough to let Tevis and his pals catch up with them, and by then Sharrock would be out of here. There was one man he'd come here to find, and that sonofabitch should pay for everything.

'Let's go, fellers,' Sharrock said. He touched heels, and the appaloosa moved forward into the blinding swirls of snow, the huge dog trotting alongside man and horse as they headed deeper into the timber. Guiding his mount between the dark boles of the pines, Sharrock smiled tightly, satisfied for the moment. Nightfall should see them out from this wooded stretch, and after that the trail led clear on to Kimball's Point.

Come daylight, he'd be there, he thought.

★ ★ ★

He waited at a point off the trail where the timber stood thickest, pressed up close to the frozen pine trunk with his booted legs ankle-deep in the piling drifts. Anderson kept a hold on the long halter-rope, his free hand covering the muzzle of the fretting bay gelding, whose breath sent white streamers into the air. Snowfall was getting worse by the minute, coating him with a layer of white as flakes pelted at eyes and ears and mouth. The dark man shivered in spite of his heavy clothing, he knew that it wasn't just from the cold. He'd been feverish since he left Riggott behind, and should never have left town with his wounds unhealed. But the way Anderson saw it, he didn't have time to waste. Not if he aimed to do the job he was here for.

The schoolma'am had insisted on tending his wounds, back at the station house. Her name was Helena Sibley, and whatever her Ma had taught her, he reckoned she'd learned mighty well. She'd used his hunting-knife to dig out the shotgun slugs from his hip and shoulder, heating the blade and cleaning the wounds with whiskey from one of the drummer's samples that stung like fire, but had done the job. Like he'd figured, she'd been the hardest to convince that he had to leave.

Helena Sibley had watched as Canfield and the porter had helped fix his saddle and gear on the bay horse, and stood back to let him climb awkwardly aboard.

'Yours is a foolhardy venture, Mr Rankin,' the teacher informed him. Over the spectacles, those steely eyes had fixed him with the most severe stare they could muster. 'You are risking your life to no good purpose, believe me. I only hope you do not have cause to regret it.'

'If you say so, ma'am.' Anderson had touched the brim of his hat, easing rein as he turned the bay around. 'Thanks all the same, Miss Sibley. Same goes for all the rest of you folks here.'

'Good luck, Mr Rankin,' Helena

Sibley said. Her voice was echoed by Canfield and the rest. Anderson had raised his hand to them as the gelding stepped away across the icy station yard. He hadn't looked back.

★　★　★

He felt the bay horse fret and fidget against his hand, and knew he didn't have long to wait. Minutes later the crunch of hoofs on hard-packed snow gave further warning, and horse and rider loomed into sight against the blanketing fall of white. Something else came trotting beside them. A huge dog, its fur a thick, brindled grey, whose shaggy head reached high against the horse's flank. Anderson drew in his breath sharply, his free hand easing down to rest on the butt of the holstered .45 Colt. A dog was something he hadn't figured on, and this one was bigger than any he'd seen in his life. Anderson had heard the shooting and made sure he and the gelding stood some distance off the trail, downwind of any passing rider, but a dog was different. You never could figure what they'd do next.

His gaze touched on the horse and rider, and at once his face hardened, right hand tightening its grip on the pistol butt. The horse was a fine-looking animal, its white coat spotted with black hand-sized patches and, like the dog, Anderson hadn't seen it before. It was the man astride it who interested him most. Anderson fixed on the rider, looking him over with a grey, flinty stare. The horseman was slender and small, his slim frame undisguised by the thick coat he wore. The wide-brimmed hat was pulled low on his brow, and he'd hauled up the collar of the jacket to protect his ears, but from here Anderson could see him plain. Against the white of the snowfall the features showed thin and fierce as those of a hawk, the flesh smooth and ebony black. A tough, ruthless face, thin-lipped and high-cheekboned. One he'd seen before, and didn't aim to forget.

'Sharrock.' Anderson barely breathed the word. He stayed watching as the horseman went by them, going on along the trail at a steady walk. Sharrock's dark eyes raked the trees around as he rode, but Anderson had picked his spot well, and that look didn't find them. Beside his master, the giant dog sniffed the air, shaking his head against the falling snowflakes, and growled low in his throat. Anderson was ready to pull the Colt loose when the rider turned in the saddle, calling out.

'C'mon, Abe!' Sharrock shouted. 'Quit foolin', you hear? We got work to do!'

Abe had his muzzle pointed in Anderson's direction, growling still as he sniffed the air. The sound of Sharrock's voice decided him, and the big dog turned away, loping to keep pace with horse and man as they headed deeper into the timber. Pretty soon the three of them were lost from sight.

The cold was eating into him, and it was an effort to control the shaking of his body. Anderson pawed wet snow-flakes from his face and eased cautiously away from the pine bole, moving his gloved hand from the muzzle of the bay. For a while he stood, holding the animal by its long rein, his dark Indian features troubled as he scanned the woods around him. Anderson had seen some gunfight-ers in his time, but they didn't come any more deadly than Lee Sharrock. Right now he was thinking about the last time they'd met, and how lucky he'd been to come out ahead. Way he saw it, a man could push his luck too far in that line of work, and maybe that was what he was doing now.

It was a surprise he could have done without, finding Sharrock this far north, and headed in what looked like the same direction. Any way he viewed it, this was about to make his job a whole lot tougher.

He waited another half-hour or so before getting ready to move. Anderson was set to mount up when the gelding snorted and shied, ears pricking forward, and he knew they had company. The dark man covered the horse's muzzle, going flat to the pine trunk again as the sound of other hoofs crunched on the icy trail. He was into cover in time to watch the three horsemen ride by above him. Three *hombres* in thick, fur-lined jackets and heavy cords, the hats pulled low over their faces as they pushed forward, heads down against the snowfall. All three rode slowly, looking tired and beat and angry, and maybe they had reason. Eyeing the steam that rose off the flanks of the horses, the heavy breaths that smoked in the chill air, Anderson figured the critters had been run or ridden kind of hard. Sharrock should have no trouble staying clear of them, he thought.

The feller in the lead was big and heavy-set, with a flushed, hot colour to his face. A little, ferret-featured *hombre* followed close behind, while riding drag came a lanky, hard-favoured jasper, tall and thin as a fence-rail. There wasn't a smile to be had from one of them, all three scowling and shoving their tired mounts forward, like they couldn't wait to get out of these woods and be someplace else. Thankfully, none of them spared a glance to the spot below where he and the bay stood in cover of the pines. Tired or not, Anderson reckoned he wasn't in the best shape for a shoot-out at odds of three to one.

He frowned, watching their fur-coated backs out of sight as men and horses vanished into the snowfall and the darkening shadow of the trees. Anderson had never set eyes on these men before. Like the shotgun-toting gunhawks at the station, they were strangers to him. Somehow, though, he had the feeling he'd be meeting them again before he was through.

Right now he needed to get out of these woods, and quickly. His wounds and the cold had left him in bad shape, and if anything the snow was coming down harder than ever. Anderson knew if he stayed out here he'd freeze to death by morning. Then again, with Sharrock and the three other riders headed the same way as himself, he figured his chances weren't likely to be much better once he made Kimball's Point. Anderson shrugged wearily, flinched as the raw chill cut into his bones. No choice for him now but to go ahead, and do the best he could.

The bay horse snorted, shifting away from him as he approached. The critter could feel the way he shivered, sensed his weariness. Like him, it knew Anderson was at the end of his rope.

He mounted with an effort, ducked his head to the swirling snow.

Staying clear of the trail, he nudged the gelding forward along the foot of the slope and into the next dense stand of pines. All the same, he couldn't help but think of Sharrock as he rode, and one question kept cropping up in his mind.

The dead men back at the station

had known enough to be ready and waiting for him. Chances were the same was true for the three *hombres* in the woods. But one way and another, it hadn't worked out for them.

Had Sharrock been a surprise for them too, he wondered.

3

The appaloosa horse stood hitched outside Huber's saloon, pawing with one forehoof at the thick, frozen mud of a potholed track that saw duty as the town's one and only street. Hearing the crunch of other oncoming hoofs, the animal turned its head and drew a long, steaming breath, peering into the darkness towards them. As if it had known all along they were coming, and was none too surprised to see them.

'He's here right enough, the sonofabitch,' Bull Tevis said. He drew rein, holding in the big sorrel horse as it stamped and hauled against the rope. The other two riders pulled up behind him. For a while the three of them sat their mounts, shoulders hunched to the flurrying snow as they eyed the tethered horse, and the dull glow from the saloon window that threw a yellow wedge of light on the nearest of the drifts outside.

'His hoss, all right,' Pete Crow's voice was sour, the thin features clenched into a scowl. Maybe it had something to do with the gash the stranger's bullet had cut along his ribs, before they made it out of the woods. Tevis and Fairchild had bound the wound with strips from his flannel undershirt, but the little gunman still carried himself kind of stiff in the saddle, and his friends knew better than to cross him in his present mood. 'So where's the goddamn dog, huh? Sure be a pleasure to ventilate that critter's hide!'

Tevis said nothing, his thick bull neck buried deep in his collar as he studied the appaloosa, his eyes pale and murderous in the red beef of his face.

'Just who the hell is he, anyhow?' Charlie Fairchild wanted to know. He leaned his gaunt frame on the neck of his mount, the last of the saloon light striking on his hard-planed, hollow-cheeked features. Fairchild's eyes still stung raw from the bark sprayed into them, and every now and then he would swat at them with the back of a wet-gloved hand.

'Don't rightly know, Charlie,' Crow answered sullenly, one hand itching on the butt of the Smith & Wesson .44 that nestled butt forward in his belt. 'Don't care too much, neither. Any rider comes up through the woods, we take 'em down. Ain't that what he told us?'

'Yeah, Pete. That's what he said.' Bull Tevis shook his massive head against the pelting snow, swore as he slapped the flakes from his face. The big man unbuttoned his coat, shoving it back to lay a hand on the pistol holstered on his right hip, flicked off the rawhide thong that held the hammer down. 'Tell you somethin' else, boys. Ain't no black son born that plays Bull Tevis for a fool, an' goes on breathin' after. I aim to make that bastard pay, you hear?'

In the silence that followed, Crow and Fairchild frowned, thinking it over.

'Better make sure this time, I reckon,'

the gaunt man offered. For now, he made no move to loosen his coat, still lying on the horse's neck as he scanned the street with raw, bloodshot eyes. 'What you figure he's gonna say, once he gets to hear about it?'

'Ain't gonna go down well with Magruder neither,' Crow said. At once big Tevis rounded on him, anger and impatience in his voice.

'The hell with Magruder!' The thickset *hombre* tightened his hold on the pistol-butt, spitting out the words. 'It's the Big Man we gotta worry about!'

'How 'bout this Anderson feller?' Fairchild still sounded curious. 'Looks like he ain't gonna show, don't it?'

'Don't worry, Charlie. He won't.' Tevis chuckled, an ugly sound that grated in his fat, wattled throat. 'Croft an' Freeman know their business. They'll have fixed him good, I reckon. Now all we have to do is what we shoulda done the last time, an' put paid to this sonofabitch. If you fellers are ready, I vote we pay him a call right now.'

'I'm with you, Bull,' Pete Crow told him. On the far side of him, Fairchild eased his gaunt frame upright in the saddle, and nodded.

'So let's do it, boys,' Bull Tevis said. The big man glared savagely into the darkness as he spoke. 'And this time, no mistakes.'

He touched hooks to send the sorrel forward, the others following in silence. Snow fell heavily as they emerged from the trees, coating men and horses with a sheath of white. The horsemen skirted the edge of the woods, avoiding the light from the saloon to make for the feed barn, which threw a deeper shadow at the far end of the street. By the time the three of them hauled rein around the long wall of the building, Crow and Tevis had already drawn their guns.

Sitting his mount maybe twenty yards back into the pine woods, Anderson watched them go. The tall man held rein on the fretting bay, keen eyes peering through the snowfall as the three dark shapes left the shelter of the trees, heading for the barn at the end of the street. Seemed to him their outlines began to blur as he tried to keep them in sight, and he found himself lurching forward in the saddle. Anderson swore, steadying himself with his free hand against the high saddle horn, and felt the impact strike a fiery pain from his shoulder. His right arm was stiff, awkward and heavy as a log, and the pain in his hip wasn't much better. In spite of the cold he sweated hard, and the shivering was so bad it felt like he was about to shake himself apart. Just as well the town was right ahead, he doubted if he'd have made another mile in this shape. Only trouble was, the company had arrived before him.

Hard to figure what to do next. Anderson was fairly sure that the three horsemen weren't around to improve his health. Where Sharrock fitted into all this he couldn't tell, but right now that didn't matter. Feverish as he was, and close to collapse, Anderson needed to make sure he had the drop on them. And that meant that he, too, had to move.

He prodded heels to his mount, and the bay stepped out for the edge of the trees. Anderson didn't follow the three riders, instead striking away to the left, hugging the fringe of the woods to head down a snow-covered slope that cut off the light from the saloon. Pushing the bay through deep snow, head down to the thickening flurries, he made for a narrow alleyway that led between the buildings on the street to a litter of back lots and wasteland beyond. No one saw him, and he reached it safely, man and horse shrouded in the unlit darkness. The buildings on either side threw long shadows, and only a faint light glimmered from the fallen snow.

Anderson rode the bay to the far end of the alley, and swung a leg to dismount. Down on the ground he stumbled and almost fell, righting himself against the horse's flank. With an effort he drew the heavy Colt from its holster, and looked around for a tethering-post. The nearest building sported a rickety porch, and he made the rope fast to a flimsy wooden pillar. Anderson edged around the corner, and limped towards the saloon. There had to be a back door to the place, he figured. Leastways, he hoped so.

The door was there, right enough, to the rear of the saloon. A set of wooden barrels were stacked to one side, and in front was a litter of empty and busted liquor bottles, most of them half-hidden by the snow that covered the ground. No bolt or bar, just a rusty latch to keep him out. From under the door a yellow gleam of light edged out, falling on to the snow. Maybe somebody was on the far side of that door, but it was a chance he had to take. Gun in hand, Anderson stumbled over bottles and snow and raised the latch, shoving the door. The warped wood fought him a little before it went back, groaning as it hit against the wall.

The woman in the small, dimly lit room was hoisting a couple of bottles from a crate when he lurched inside. At the sound of the door thudding back she turned around, eyes wide in shock as she stared into his face.

'What in the name of . . . ?' She was tall for a woman, he noticed, her figure lean and spare-fleshed in the shapeless calico dress with its stained leather apron. The face that met him was broad and blunt-featured, spattered with freckles, with a mane of thick, sandy hair that spilled strands over her forehead. Her eyes were a light, piercing blue, and right now they stared at him as though they didn't believe what they were seeing. Then, in an instant, shock at sight of the gun gave way to anger. 'Just what do you think you're doin' in here, mister?'

The room looked to be some kind of store, he guessed. It was stacked with barrels and wooden crates. She gave back across it as Anderson moved further inside. He saw she still gripped both of the bottles she'd been lifting, as if she didn't know how to let them go. From where she stood, she saw a tall, dark-featured man in a plaid coat and heavy cord pants, both of them stained with blood, who pointed a .45 pistol in her direction. His face looked dark enough for him to be an Indian, but the eyes were a pale, flinty grey, kind of strange in a face like his. In spite of the gun, he looked to be in bad shape, shivering all over like he had an ague, and swaying on his feet.

'Mister . . . ' For an instant her voice faltered, uncertain. 'Mister, are you all right?'

He watched her move away from him, backing towards another door that had to lead into the saloon itself. Anderson was set to follow her when he saw that shocked stare go by him for the open doorway behind. He read the warning there. Same instant it showed, he was down on the dirt floor, rolling as he fought to level the gun. Afterwards he couldn't say for sure whether he dived or fell, but either way he hit the ground in time.

Landing with a slam that knocked the breath out of him, he sensed the zip of the slug that cut air above him, and saw wood splinter off the doorframe in front. The woman gave out a kind of gasp as it struck, dropping both bottles to smash against the floor.

The tall, gaunt-featured *hombre* had come in around the back. Seemed like he and Anderson had the same thing in mind. Now he pressed up against the frame of the open door, thin face clenched tight as he lined two-handed for another shot. The weapon he held looked to be some kind of Colt, but it had the longest barrel Anderson had ever seen. He squeezed the trigger on his own .45, rolling aside as echoes of the first gunshot racketed round the cramped room. Beaten for speed, the lanky gunhawk yelled and drew back, Anderson's shot going high to gash his cheek. He fired one more time as he reeled back from the doorway, but his second try was wild, smashing into crated bottles that leaked liquor across the floor. Anderson had time for a shot of his own, but by then his target was gone from sight, and the bullet sang uselessly into the falling snow.

From inside the saloon, beyond the closed door, he heard a sudden uproar of voices, and with them the ferocious growling of a dog.

'Stay back, lady!' Anderson called. He struggled up awkwardly, gripping the wall with one hand to haul himself from the ground. The sandy-haired woman had pushed herself flat against the wall, hands clenched at her sides as if still gripping the fallen bottles. She neither spoke nor moved as he shouldered the door open, and all but fell into the larger room beyond.

The other two gunhawks had burst in from the front entrance of the saloon, whose panelled doors now hung flapping open. The big *hombre* and his ferret-faced pal ducked and weaved their way among overturned chairs and trestles, pausing to fire at a point away to his right. The rough-hewn bar was to his left, and from the corner of his eye Anderson glimpsed the crouching figure of a short, thickset feller with cropped greying hair, taking cover there. From here, he couldn't see Sharrock, or the dog. Right now, everything he saw was blurred and fuzzy at the edges, as though he was studying the saloon from underwater.

Anderson slid and lurched against the bar, fighting to hold on to the Colt. The big red-faced gunman caught the move, whipped round to send a rapid shot his way. Anderson felt pain sear like a branding-iron along the side of his head, slithered down as the blast of the gunshot hammered around the room. He hit the floor, the pistol spilling from his hand, and the big *hombre* plunged out from cover, charging in towards him with his own smoking gun lifted.

Staring up at the gun barrel and the hot, furious face above it, Anderson was all set to die when a ferocious snarling broke in on them, and a huge brindled shape came flying across the room. Bull Tevis whirled in time to raise an arm to protect his throat, yelled as powerful jaws clamped shut on his forearm. Abe's rushing onslaught slammed him back into the bar, almost knocking him off his feet. Anderson crawled feebly for his fallen gun as the big man cursed and swung around, struggling vainly to get his gun arm free of the clamping bite.

On the far side of the saloon, Lee Sharrock broke cover, dropped to one knee as he braced the .44 Remington Army over his left arm. Pete Crow reared up hurriedly over his trestle barricade, trying for a shot. Sharrock beat him by a breath, the crash of the gunshots close enough for one to echo the other. Anderson saw Sharrock flinch away for an instant, saw the ferret-faced gunman jerk straight up to full height, as if frozen in mid-air. Pete Crow went backwards and down like a falling pine, his pistol skidding from him as he hit the ground with both arms slapping wide. He didn't make a sound as he fell.

Anderson had almost made it to his own fallen .45 when Tevis ripped free of the snarling dog and clubbed at the animal's head to send it down. The big man's arm showed bloody gashes through the torn leather of the sleeve, his face a savage red mask as he pulled away to trigger in Sharrock's direction. He was already a way too late. Down on the floor, Anderson caught the stabbing of flame from the Remington Army, saw the big gunhawk go reeling back against the bar like a fighter taking punches from a grizzly bear. Sharrock's bullets knocked off a spray of dust and snow from the *hombre*'s shirt-front, drilling a couple of neat black holes just above the heart. Bull Tevis came out with a hoarse, choking sound before he stopped breathing. He sagged and toppled forward off the bar, seeming to throw the gun out ahead of him before he struck face down on the dirt floor of the saloon. It was a while before the racketing noise of gunfire died away.

'Seems like some folks just cain't be told,' Lee Sharrock said.

He got slowly to his feet, checking the pistol and fitting fresh loads as he came across the room at a lazy walk. Anderson had reached the fallen Colt, and laid his hand on the butt of the weapon. Then he saw Sharrock halt a few paces from him, and knew he hadn't a prayer.

'Just lay it down, Anderson,' the black man told him. Seeing the crop-haired man rise from behind the bar, and reach underneath it with both hands, he called out, his voice cutting sharper. 'An' you best leave that shotgun be, shorty! Already killed two, one more ain't gonna trouble me none.'

The thickset man appeared to swallow on a mighty large rock in his throat, then stepped back from the bar in a hurry, raising both hands in the air.

'That's better.' For the first time, Lee Sharrock smiled, a cold, wintry smile that cut his ebony face like a blade. He whistled to the dog, who hauled himself from the ground, shaking his shaggy head dazedly. 'Over here, Abe! They ain't killed you yet!'

The massive hound moved up against him, shoving its head at his side. Sharrock smiled bleakly, his free hand rubbing the brindled fur as he levelled the .44 Remington at the man on the ground. From outside came the noise of hoofs drumming in the hard-frozen snow. The sound of a single rider, getting out of town in a hurry.

'Guess number three just quit the game.' In spite of the smile, Sharrock's dark, high-boned face showed no hint of mercy. 'Just leaves you, Anderson, don't it?'

The ground was heaving under him, rising and falling in unsteady waves. Too far gone now even to be scared, Anderson peered up at the blurred outlines of man and gun above him, and fought to find the words.

'You aim to use that thing, best go right ahead.' Speech came out from him hoarse and slurred, as though he'd drunk so much he couldn't talk straight. Somewhere far above him, the man with the gun lost his smile.

'You reckon?' Sharrock eyed the Remington thoughtfully, shifted his glance back to the fallen man. 'Way I recall, you done me a favour one time. Could be we're even now. What you say?'

'Could be you're right.' His voice was no more than a hollow croak.

'Yeah, right.' Sharrock had lowered the pistol to his side. 'Ain't figured what the hell you're doin' in these parts, Anderson. Right now, I'm tellin' you I got business here, an' knowin' you, I reckon you just made my job a mite tougher. Best stay out of it, you hear?'

'I hear you.' Anderson barely breathed the words as the other man grew to a shimmering blur of colours above him.

'You better.' Sharrock checked the

Remington, slipped the weapon back in its holster. Turning to the undersized saloonman, he nodded.

'OK, feller, take it easy. Ain't about to kill nobody now.' As the little grey-haired *hombre* lowered his arms, the gunman moved to the bar, where a bottle and glass lay unattended. 'Thanks to these *hombres* I spilled my whiskey. Damn if I ain't gonna drink before I go.'

Back by the doorway of the store-room, Anderson heard footsteps scuff in the dirt as the woman came into the saloon behind him. He set one hand against the bar and got unsteadily to his feet, a move that sent the world turning crazily sideways. Anderson leaned against the bar, shivering as the sweat ran into his eyes.

'Your good health, lady.' Sharrock had seen the woman come in. Now he hoisted the filled glass in mock salute, still smiling coldly.

'Just get out of here, mister.' Anderson heard the tight, barely controlled anger in her voice. This one had sand all right, he thought. Maybe too much for her own good. 'We as soon not harbour killers, if it's all the same to you.'

The brief silence that followed was cold enough to freeze the blood.

'Is that right, lady?' Lee Sharrock eyed her for a moment, glanced sidelong to the two sprawling bodies on the saloon floor. He needn't have bothered. Pete Crow still lay wide-eyed and staring upward, as if trying to figure how he'd come by the black bullet-hole between those eyes. Bull Tevis remained on his face, blood from the dish-sized exit wounds spreading slowly across his back. Sharrock shrugged, turning from them. He sank the whiskey in a couple of swallows, and set down the glass.

'Much obliged, all the same. Now I'll be headed for that door, an' if you folks got sense you'll just stay watchin'.' He eased from the bar, patting the dog's shaggy head. 'C'mon, Abe. Let's go, feller.'

He crossed the saloon, stepping over

the bodies as he made for the open doors. The big hound went with him, rubbing its muzzle against his hand. When he reached the doorway, the black gunfighter turned, glancing back to Anderson.

'You want to live, stay clear,' Sharrock said. 'Come after me, Anderson, there ain't gonna be no more favours.'

Anderson didn't answer, struggling to stay on his feet. Sharrock turned around, man and dog going through the doorway and out of sight.

Suddenly the saloon was falling apart, roof and walls swooping around so fast they turned him sick. Anderson sensed the hurrying footsteps of the woman and the grey-haired man as they came towards him, heard the sound of their troubled voices. Somehow, though, it was too much of an effort to work out what the hell they were saying. He was vaguely aware of the spasm of pain that forked through his left leg, felt the limb buckle under him as strength gave out. By now he barely registered the icy blast that blew snow in through the open doors of the saloon.

The last he remembered was their arms holding on to him. Then he was diving into a black, bottomless pit that swallowed him whole, and the lights were going out.

4

He was deep in the water, the waves out of sight far above him. Anderson was fighting his way up to air and sunlight, but something seemed to press down on him, smothering the breath from his lungs as the dark waters closed in all around. It was as though he heard voices somewhere in the far distance, angry voices that snapped and quarrelled, their words too faint for his ears to catch. Anderson thought he heard one call out 'No! No!', but he couldn't be sure. Maybe it was all a dream, he figured. But the waves were real enough, filling his mouth, pushing him down as he drowned. He cried out, flailing his arms wildly, and forced himself up towards the light overhead.

He opened his eyes, and found he hadn't drowned after all. Overhead was a low, timbered roof which was lit by a hanging kerosene-lamp, and someone was fixing what felt like a pillow under his head. Anderson caught the sound of his own harsh, rapid breathing, and knew for sure that he was still alive.

'He's coming round, pa,' the young woman said.

Her breath fell gently on his face as the words were spoken, and he turned his head to the sound. Thinking it over, he was glad he'd made the effort. This one could have fitted herself into any of his dreams, and welcome, Anderson decided. The black gown with its white cuffs and collar, adorned only by a cameo brooch at the throat, served only to set off the full, womanly shape it covered. Anderson gazed up into smooth, perfect features and pale skin without a blemish, with tawny red hair that framed the face in a mane of coppery flame. Sure was worth waking up for, he thought.

'Take it easy, mister.' Her eyes were a dark, deep brown, large and enticing. They gleamed in the lamplight, echoing her smile as she finished fixing the pillow and stepped back, resting her hand for a moment on his hot forehead. 'You need to rest now.'

He didn't answer her, for the first time looking past her to the others in the room. Nearest of them was the hard-faced, sandy-haired dame from the saloon, and it seemed to Anderson she was none too pleased to have him lying there. The others stood further back, and with the lamplight in his eyes he had trouble making them out. Anderson grimaced at the pain that throbbed in neck and shoulder and hip. He glanced around, taking in the room about him, and realized that he was surrounded by the dark, oblong shapes of coffins. They filled the room, some empty with the lids laid alongside, others draped over with heavy velvet cloths. For an instant the shock of it froze him, then he pushed up from where he lay, struggling to get to his feet.

'What the . . . ?' His body was

wrapped around with bandages that smelled of some kind of ointment, and they made it hard for him to move. Anderson was ready to swear when he met that gentle, reassuring smile, and lay back again. 'Beggin' your pardon, lady, but maybe somebody kin tell me just what I'm doin' here?'

'Certainly, my dear sir.' Another figure loomed forward into the light, the two women giving back to let him by. The man was tall, with a slender but broad-shouldered build. Anderson guessed that the *hombre* probably matched him for size, but this close the black-clad figure seemed to rear to a spectral height above him. 'Allow me to explain, Mr . . . ?'

'Rankin. Joshua Rankin.' Anderson knew it came out too quickly.

'Jordan Hemphill, at your service.' The tall man bowed, extending a hand. His voice was sonorous and deep, the pale features set in a grave expression, and he was rigged to match, his lofty frame sheathed in black broadcloth coat and pants, starched white shirt with a stiff collar, set off with a black string necktie. 'A pleasure to make your acquaintance, Mr Rankin, even under these adverse circumstances.'

'You'll be the undertaker here, right?' Anderson used his unwounded left hand, felt the strength of the other man's grasp.

'You are, of course, correct.' For the first time, Hemphill managed the faintest of smiles. Scanning the strong, aquiline face, Anderson guessed he was handsome in a pale, serious kind of way. The grey hair that looked like it had once been red was cut short, plastered flat to his skull with pomade, the moustache neatly trimmed. Meeting the intent gaze of those pale-blue eyes, Anderson was startled to find a resemblance with the woman from the saloon. 'The others here are family also. My daughters — this is Kedron, my youngest.'

He indicated the pretty redhead, who smiled winningly down at him. Anderson reckoned that smile could have melted the ice clear off the roofs outside.

'Glad to know you, Miss Hemphill.' It cost him no trouble to sound as though he meant it, and that got him another smile.

'It's my pleasure, Mr Rankin,' Kedron told him.

'Abigail, my eldest.' Hemphill nodded towards the lean, hard-looking female. Seemed to Anderson he quit smiling that same instant. 'I believe the two of you have already met?'

'That's right.' Anderson glanced towards the elder daughter, and was met by a fierce, withering stare from those pale eyes that so closely matched her father's. 'Miss Hemphill.'

'Mr Rankin.' Abigail made no attempt to smile, swiping a hand at the sandy hair that fell over her face. Reading her fierce expression, Hemphill quickly indicated the young man who now stepped forward to join him.

'And this is Gilead, my only son.'

'A pleasure, Mr Rankin.' Gilead

Hemphill leaned forward to shake hands. Garbed in black like his father, he lacked Jordan Hemphill's height, standing medium tall with a slender, almost girlish build. He had the same fiery hair and dark eyes as Kedron, and just like her he had more good looks than anyone had a right to. 'Glad to see you are recovering.'

'Goes for me too, Mr Hemphill,' Anderson said.

'We brought you over here after the . . . unpleasantness in the saloon.' Jordan Hemphill's features wrinkled in distaste, and he glanced reprovingly in Abigail's direction. 'Not that I frequent such places myself, you understand. I took the pledge many years ago, and have eschewed the demon drink ever since. It has always been my wish that my family should do the same.' Reading the smouldering anger in his daughter's gaze, he smiled and went on: 'Forgive me, Mr Rankin. As I was saying, we brought you here, and laid you on this bed, which is my own. My work often requires my presence here overnight, you understand.' Eyeing the ranked coffins all around, he spoke more softly. 'The two — deceased gentlemen were also accomodated here. I trust you do not mind?'

'Not if I ain't about to join 'em.' Anderson flexed his right arm, grimaced to the answering twinge of pain. By now, though, he reckoned it didn't feel so bad.

'You were suffering from a fever,' Hemphill was saying. 'No doubt this was the result of exposure and the wounds you appear to have suffered from a previous encounter. They were not fully healed, and with your later exertions in the saloon, small wonder you should have succumbed.' He smiled again, waving a hand as if to dismiss the memory. 'Fortunately, I have some skill in medical matters, having studied briefly in that line before adopting my current profession. I was able to treat your injuries, and with rest and recuperation, a few days should see you fully restored to health.'

'That's good to know, Mr Hemphill.' Anderson sounded thoughtful. 'Just how long have I been here, you reckon?'

'It was last night when we brought you here,' the undertaker told him. 'The fever broke soon afterwards. You have slept through most of the day since then.' Glancing to the two women, he smiled more fondly. 'My daughters nursed you through the crisis. Kedron, I believe, was particularly attentive.'

'Mighty grateful to you, ma'am.' Anderson nodded his thanks, and Kedron gave him that smile that set his insides melting.

'Think nothing of it, Mr Rankin,' the redhead told him. Behind her Abigail said nothing, raking the man on the bed with a cold, unforgiving stare. Sure as hell hadn't made a hit with her, he thought.

'Mighty obliged, all the same,' Anderson said.

Hemphill was set to speak again,

when someone hammered on the door at the far end of the funeral parlour, and they heard the slam as it burst open. The little crop-haired *hombre* bustled in and pulled up sharply as he sighted the group around the bed.

'Beggin' your pardon, Jordan, but it's hottin' up back there. Just comin' to see if Abby was still over here.' Seeing Anderson watching him from the bed, his voice tailed off, and he forced a grin. 'Howdy, feller. Looks like you're on the mend, huh?'

'So they tell me.' Anderson found a faint smile of his own. 'Joshua Rankin.'

'Mr Rankin.' This close, Anderson saw his hair wasn't grey, but a white ash-blond, cropped short to the skull. The features were brown and weather-beaten, the eyes a boyish cornflower blue. For an instant the little man hesitated, frowning as he heard the name. Then he grinned again, holding out a red, hard-skinned hand.

'Huber, Carl Huber. Call me Dutchy

if you like, everybody else does around here.'

'Glad to know you, Dutchy.' Anderson held on to his smile. From above them both, Jordan Hemphill spoke again.

'Mr Huber runs the saloon across the street, where my daughter Abigail finds employment.' The undertaker made no attempt to hide the disapproval in his voice. 'He has been kind enough to agree to look after your horse.' He paused, studying the man on the bed more cautiously, it seemed. 'I took the liberty of handing your weapons into his care for the present. I hope you don't mind.'

For a while Anderson stayed quiet, thinking it over. Suddenly he realized why he felt so naked.

'I abhor violence, Mr Rankin, as do my family.' Hemphill's sepulchral voice wouldn't have been out of place in a pulpit. He treated Anderson to a severe look as he parted with the words. 'You are a welcome guest, but I'll have no firearms in this house, if it's all the same to you.'

'Your house, Mr Hemphill.' Anderson tried a shrug, flinched as a dull ache answered from his shoulder. 'Your rules, I reckon.'

'Naturally, they will be returned to you once you are fully recovered.' Hemphill made sure Anderson knew how much he didn't approve.

Huber felt the uncomfortable silence that followed, and hurried to break it.

'Got your gear back at the saloon yonder, Mr Rankin.' The saloonman sounded impressed. 'Mighty pretty Winchester you got there, an' that Colt pistol too. Favour a Texas saddle, I see.'

'That's right.'

'Your bay hoss is a good enough critter.' The little man frowned, turning the thought for a while. 'Not up to that appaloosa the other feller was ridin', mind. He a friend of yours, Mr Rankin?'

'Guess not.' Anderson shook his

head. 'Met up with him once before, is all.'

'Uhuh.' Huber didn't sound too sure. 'Well, gotta git back there, I guess.' He looked towards the scowling figure of Abigail, his voice uncertain. 'You comin', Abby? Likely to be real busy in a while.'

'Just give me a minute, Dutchy, all right?' The sandy-haired woman still had her eyes fixed on Anderson. 'I'd appreciate a word with Mr Rankin here.'

'Whatever you say, Abby.' Huber shrugged, flashed a grin at the man on the bed. 'Be seein' you, feller.'

He turned, heading back through the door, which he'd left open behind him. Hearing it slam shut, Abigail met the combined, questioning stares of the other three as they turned towards her.

'That's right.' Her own fierce gaze didn't waver, the sound of her voice coming hard as a hatchet. 'I'd like a word with Mr Rankin. A private word, if you don't mind.'

Hemphill held with that stare for a moment, frowning as though he might just hand out a scolding, or maybe even some of that violence he abhorred. Then the tall man drew a steadying breath, and nodded.

'As you wish, Abigail.' He made the name sound like an insult. The undertaker bowed curtly in Anderson's direction. 'Allow me to wish you a speedy recovery, Mr Rankin. Until then, you may be sure we shall do our best for you. Come Kedron, Gilead. Your sister wishes to be alone with our guest.'

He left the bedside, moving back across the room, the other two following. Kedron lagged behind a little, Anderson noticed, as if she was none too keen to leave. She favoured him with one last, smiling glance before the three of them reached the door, and went outside.

'You an' me need to talk, Mr Rankin,' Abigail said. She moved in closer, seating herself at the side of the bed. Looking up into those pale eyes, he found them as cold and hard as before.

'Or should I say Mr Anderson?' the sandy-haired woman wanted to know. 'It's what the black feller called you, ain't it? An' Dutchy Huber heard it, too.'

'Yes, ma'am. That's what he called me.' Anderson's dark Indian face stayed expressionless as he answered.

'An' meantime you're tellin' everybody here your name's Rankin?' Abigail had trouble controlling the anger in her voice.

'That's right.'

'Pardon me if I don't believe you — Mr Anderson!'

'Reckon that's your choice, Miss Abigail.' Anderson, too, had begun to sound impatient. 'One thing I want to say, Miss Abigail, an' that's thanks. If you hadn't looked by me that way, back of the saloon, that feller would have nailed me for sure. I'd like you to know I appreciate that.'

'Don't thank me, Mr — whatever your name is!' She slapped back the falling lock of hair, her freckled features flushing hot. 'That man startled me, just the same as you did, that's all. I certainly didn't mean to help you, or your killer friend in the saloon!'

'Told you already, Sharrock ain't no friend of mine.' Anderson sighed wearily, meeting that angry blue gaze as best he could. 'You saw him pull a gun on me, so did Huber.'

'He's a gunfighter, isn't he.' Abigail's look still accused him. 'And you are also a gunfighter, ain't you, Mr So-called Rankin.'

'Not the way he is, ma'am.'

'Seems to me the two of you are very much alike.' The sandy-haired woman spoke contemptuously, getting up from the bed. For a while she stood, arms folded, glaring down at him. 'When a feller can't talk straight to me, I don't have no time for him. Whoever you are, mister, you got somethin' to hide, an' that don't bode well.'

'Miss Abigail.' Anderson held with that fierce stare as he answered. 'I didn't come here to harm you or your folks, an' that's the truth.'

'If you say so, Mr Rankin.' Abigail shook her head, unconvinced. The tall woman turned from him, moving away towards the door. Half-way there she halted, looking back.

'I nursed you when you were sick, just the same as Kedron did,' she told the man on the bed. 'Long as you're a guest in this house, I'll do my best to get you well an' out of here. What I know I'll keep to myself for now, an' Dutchy won't talk, but that's where it ends. Best you remember I know you're a liar an' a killer both, an' I got no time for you. Understood?'

'I hear you, Miss Abigail.'

'Goodnight, Mr Rankin.'

He watched the door close quietly behind her, leaving him alone in the room. Anderson breathed out slowly, sinking back on the bed, frowning as he stared at the lamplit ceiling. Abigail could be trouble in a while, he figured.

For now, though, he had no choice but to stay here until he was fit to ride. No need to hurry, either. Whoever the folks were that he was up against, they'd been expecting him from the start, and there was no way he'd spring any surprises by arriving sooner. Should they come looking for him now, he'd just have to play it the best he could.

Right now other thoughts than of Abigail, or even her pretty sister, troubled his mind. Just what the hell was Sharrock doing out here? Where did he fit into all this? Then again, who had sent word on ahead that meant Anderson found two *hombres* with shotguns waiting for him at the Riggott station? And who was the big wheel behind it all, who'd brought him this far north in the first place?

Too many questions without answers, and the aching weariness of his body tugged at him, dragging him down into sleep. Anderson closed his eyes, letting the darkness claim him. Come morning, it might just be better, he thought.

One last question clung with him before he slept.

How long would it be before they tried for him again?

5

'Nothin' movin' down there,' Theo Magruder said.

He leaned back into the massive cedar trunk, the single lens held to his eye as he peered into the rain. Beyond the cedar woodland the slope went down through moss and rotting dead-falls to where the river ran clear between stands of willows, heading for the ocean. And by the river lay the open stretch of ground that housed the settlement.

Rain came in from seaward, sweeping the village and the land around in a slow, scything downpour that ham-mered spray from the mud and the fallen trees, speckling the river as it moved inland. Boughs of the tall cedars above the slope kept off the worst of it, but it came spattering through all the same. Warm, heavy droplets that struck on the back of his neck and on the upturned faces of the men who waited with him, slapping to earth on leaves and litter. Somewhere behind the downpour, the grey rolling mass that was the Pacific Ocean surged in for the land, and fell back again.

Magruder ignored it, squinting through raindrops that swam across the lens of the old Army spyglass to the village below. The glass brought the whole place closer in spite of the rain. Through that artificial eye, Magruder saw the huge plank-built houses with their painted bird figures on walls and doors. Huge thirty-foot dugout canoes lay beached and untended by the riverside, and fronting the houses a dozen or so totem poles stood in a solid rank, towering skywards. Each post swarmed with strange carved shapes that yelled silently from their fanged and beaked mouths. Heads of eagles and snakes, birds and critters he'd never set eyes on before. There was even some kind of crazy fish that bared a set of teeth. Magruder took another look and let out a harsh breath, lowering the spyglass. This place was enough to give any civilized feller the shivers, he thought.

'See the smoke yonder?' Etheridge prodded a finger to where the grey skeins drifted upward, scattering to the onset of the rain. The little, leather-faced gunman scowled, shoved the hat back on his thumb-smooth skull to flip rainwater from the brim. 'Bastards are there, right enough.'

'That I already figured.' Magruder was running out of patience, and his quirt-lash answer showed it. 'Still ain't makin' no move, neither.'

'They won't,' Joel Deacon said. He squatted down on the other side of the outlaw boss, huddled on his haunches against a cedar bole, his collar upturned to the spattering rain. Deacon glanced up as Magruder turned to look his way, meeting the glare of his leader without so much as a blink. It was a habit Magruder had never cared for all the time he'd known him.

'You reckon?' Right now, Magruder looked as mean as he sounded. Deacon, though, didn't move a muscle.

'I know so.' Deacon's eyes were dark, almost black in the pale, smooth-shaven face. They held coldly on the bigger man as he answered. 'You're forgettin' I worked out here before, Theo. Injuns in these parts don't hunt this time of year. Bunch of 'em hole up like bears once winter hits. Ain't gonna come outa there till the spring.'

'Is that right?' Magruder scratched at his grey, glistening beard, eyeing the other man as he would a lobo wolf. Deacon was dark-haired and slender, no more than average height. Standing up, he wouldn't have reached the chest of the big, rawboned man glaring down at him. Everything about Joel Deacon looked plain and ordinary and hardly worth a mention, but Magruder knew better. He'd seen that same untroubled look on the dark *hombre*'s face as he shot down the three Indian boys they'd met further south a few weeks back, and knew that Deacon was colder than a rattler, with icewater running in his veins. There were times he scared Magruder, too.

'That's right.' Deacon's face stayed impassive as he answered.

'We gonna sit here talkin' it over, or do somethin'?' That was Joey Creed, cutting in uninvited from the bunch behind them. 'This rain gits much worse, gonna drown before we git off a shot.'

Magruder turned his head slowly, taking in the speaker at his back. Creed was no more than a kid, eighteen or nineteen at best, blond and blue-eyed, the soft golden down that furred his face not worth the trouble to shave. Magruder eyed the fancy two-gun rig the youngster had strapped over his sodden mackinaw, the plated Colt pistols with their ebony butts. Slowly, his glance came up into that angry, boyish face.

'Gonna have your chance real soon,

kid,' the big man said. 'Meantime, hush your mouth, OK? Or maybe you reckon you're runnin' this show?'

Hit by the fierce, grey-eyed stare, Creed's face flushed and turned sullen. He shut his mouth tight, shaking his head.

'Good enough,' Magruder said. He shifted his glance from the kid to where the other waiting men huddled in their wet slickers which glistened under the rain, hands impatient at pistols and carbines. Jeb Callander, massive and ox-shouldered, the red beard fanning out over his barrel chest. Hiram Beard, short and squat as a boulder, his dark face striped by the long white knife-scar that joined his lip to his ear. The thin, stooping figure of Cage Ireson, mousy-haired and scowling as he scratched the smallpox marks that pitted his cheeks. Fifteen gunhands, every one a man-killer, and mean as hell. Every one knowing Theo Magruder was meaner yet. 'Goes for you fellers too, ain't that so?'

Scowls and mutterings answered him, but that was all. Nobody, not even Creed, was dumb enough to tell him different.

'That's what I figured.' Magruder had begun to smile. The big, rawboned *hombre* turned from them, his look coming back to the men on either side. 'OK, Deacon, I hear what you're tellin' me, an' it makes no never mind. Just have to smoke 'em out, is all. How many of 'em, you reckon?'

'Not so much.' Deacon shrugged his shoulders, spraying water with the move. 'Village ain't no more than thirty, forty at most. I'd say a dozen fighting men, rest is oldsters, squaws an' kids. An' they ain't fighters, neither. These are peaceable folk.' He paused, eyeing the taller man with a faint, mocking smile. 'Our kind of Injuns, Theo.'

'Guns?' Magruder's voice was flat and hard. Eyes still on the grey-bearded face above him, Deacon chuckled and shook his head.

'A few, maybe.' The dark man pushed

himself up from the ground, rainwater sluicing off his slickered back. 'Nothin' to trouble over. Most of 'em, it's gonna be harpoons, axes an' knives. An' they don't come as quick as a pistol slug.'

He reached under the coat, drawing his gun from the holster. Magruder said nothing, watching Deacon smile coldly at sight of the weapon, a Colt .36 Navy, its walnut grip shiny with wear. Neat, well-balanced pistol, the kind a marksman would use. Or a killer, like the man who held it now. The bearded man turned from him, fished the spyglass from his pocket. For a while he scanned the village again, studying the houses, the beached dugouts, the looming totem poles.

'Fellers,' he told the men behind him, 'we know why we're out here. Those Injuns down there got what we're after, an' we're about to go take it. From what I hear, shipment's due inside a week, an' when it comes we'll be ready.' He stowed the spyglass, glancing to Etheridge as his voice lashed harder.

'Cal, take five men an' cut through the woods around the back. I want them smoke-holes blocked, you hear?'

'I hear you, Theo.' The little *hombre* nodded, raindrops gleaming where they caught and hung in the gullied runnels of his face. He called out to the waiting gunmen, pointing to his choices.

'OK, Beard, you're with me. You too, Jeb, an' Zach, Pete an' Sturgess. Let's be goin', boys.'

He stumbled away through the trees, the others hurrying to follow. Rain struck on them through the boughs as they made off, their figures dwarf-like against the towering cedar trunks all around.

'First shot we hear, we'll be down!' Magruder called after them.

He reached behind him to where the American Arms shotgun stood ready against the cedar-bole. The big man grasped the weapon, noting the single sawn-down barrel approvingly. Shotgun did the job, he found, and Magruder never had liked to fight from a distance.

Close quarters had always suited him best.

'Unleather them pistols, fellers,' Magruder told them. 'Those Injuns gonna be out any time now, an' soon as they show, we're gonna hit 'em with everything we got. Do this right, we oughta finish the job in one.'

Beside him Joel Deacon didn't speak, eyes on the village as he stroked the barrel of the Colt. Magruder eyed the pale, stoney-smooth features, his frown returning. Gunhawks and killers he'd met in plenty, but this one was different. Maybe his being a Canuck had something to do with it, the big man thought. Word was that Deacon had gunned down a trapper in Manitoba someplace, and skipped Stateside when the Mounties came after him. Since then Deacon had been working with the organization, and knowing the country north of the line like he did, he'd been mighty helpful. All the same, there were times he made Magruder uneasy.

Magruder's brother had wound up in a Canadian jail after one of the Fenian raids around the Great Lakes a few years back. He didn't care for Canucks, or their British friends, any more than he relished a diamondback's bite. Right now, though, he didn't aim to tell Deacon what was on his mind.

He was still thinking it over when he saw Etheridge and his group break cover, coming out from the cedar woods directly above the village. Just as he'd figured, the route they'd taken brought them almost in reach of the roofs of those plank houses, and as he watched Beard and the others moved in to pitch thick bundles of litter and brush down on to the smoke-holes. The drifting whorls faded, smothered by the brush. In his mind, Theo Magruder saw the sudden rush of smoke flooding back into the plank houses, blinding and choking those inside.

'That oughta do it,' the big man muttered.

From below a startled yelling broke

the hiss of the downpour, and the doors of the houses burst open. Half-naked figures plunged into the open, choking and spluttering for breath from the smoke that billowed out behind them. None of them paid any mind to the rain that hammered them as they fought to rub the smoke from reddening eyes. As they came into sight he glimpsed the first telltale stabs of flame from the cedars on the right, and a ragged blast of gunfire ripped through the yelling and the sound of the falling rain.

'Let's go!' Magruder shouted.

He led them downhill at a run, his booted feet slithering in moss and crumbling litter as the shots rang out again. Etheridge and the others were in the open now, taking careful aim and picking their targets. The Indians were running everywhere, those who weren't already down and dying in the mud. He saw Joel Deacon line his .36 Colt on a fleeing squaw, watched the woman dive forward into the ground as the slug took the top off her head. The Canuck had it right, they were mostly oldsters and squaws and kids. Only a handful stood to fight, and they didn't have a hope in hell. Magruder swung the shotgun to take in the group and triggered, snarled approval as three men armed with fishing spears went spilling down to the scything blast of buckshot. This shouldn't take too long, he thought.

He crammed in fresh loads, firing again as the guns of Creed and the rest crashed from around him, blowing away all other sounds.

Black, oily smoke swirled out from the open doors of the houses. It trailed across the open ground, hanging like a mist, as guns barked and bodies fell and the endless rain hammered down.

It was still falling when the strewn corpses lay quiet at last, and the echoes of the final gunshots died away.

6

The busted tomato can went flying, plugged clean through as it leapt from its perch on top of the fence-post. The heavy slam of the gunshot followed in the moment it hit the ground. Anderson didn't wait to see it, gripping the Colt left-handed as he shifted aim for the next one along. One after the other he watched them fall, springing off the posts of the sagging, lopsided rail fence to land in muddy slush. Five cans, five hits. The dark man flicked out the gate and shucked the dead shells, reloaded before transferring the pistol to his right hand.

'Mighty fine shootin', Rankin!' Dutchy Huber stepped past him, walking through slush and melting snow to where the spilled cans lay punctured on the ground. The crop-haired saloonman grinned, setting them back on the posts, and came hurriedly back out of the line of fire. 'I'd say you're used to handlin' that there pistol, feller. Ain't that so?'

'Reckon you're right, Huber.' Anderson weighed the gun cautiously in his right hand, felt the answering twinge in his shoulder. Thanks to Hemphill and his daughters, the wounds were healed up by now. Only an itching scab remained from the gash on his neck, and a touch of stiffness in his hip and shoulder. All the same, this was the first time he'd touched the Colt since the shootout in the saloon. 'A while back, I was a scout with the Army. Since then, well, let's say there's been times I've known it come in kind of handy.'

'That's what I figured.' Huber stood back, still grinning as he folded both arms across his chest. Behind them both came the crash and slither of snow that slid from the eaves of the saloon and the neighbouring buildings along the street. The weather had turned milder now, the once-frozen ground thawing to a quagmire of mud and slush that broke down into puddles here and there. 'Name's Dutchy, by the way. Seem to recall I told you that before.'

'Have it your way, Dutchy.' It was Anderson's turn to grin. Already he felt much better. With the thaw, the old wound in his left leg had quit paining him, and pretty soon he figured he'd be ready to ride. 'Always found it pays if you kin shoot with either hand. Let's see how it works out this time, huh?'

'Checked out them other pistols in your saddle-bags, too.' Huber's voice touched on him before he had raised the gun. As usual, the saloonman was curious. 'Remington an' LeMat, an' then the Colt an' the Winchester carbine. Looks like you come up well-heeled to Idaho, Mr Rankin.'

'Can't be too careful, Dutchy.' Anderson didn't turn his head, lifting the pistol. 'That's how I see it.'

'Sometimes pays not to give the right name neither, I guess.'

'Could be you're right.' The dark man lowered the Colt, turning to glance back to the shorter figure behind him. 'All I kin tell you is, I got my reasons, Dutchy. An' I ain't runnin' from the law, neither, if that's what you're thinkin'.'

'Reckon I believe you, Rankin.' Huber's round face had grown thoughtful. 'Ain't so sure 'bout that Sharrock feller, mind.'

'Goes for me too, Dutchy,' Anderson said.

He took aim at the nearest of his targets, and pressed the trigger. Anderson shifted sideways as the roar of the gun came back to them, following the line of cans on their posts. Stiffness in the right arm hampered him a little, and he missed the second one, but steadied his aim to bring down the rest. One can sat glinting on the fence in the watery sunshine as the other four rolled in the mud. Eyeing the results of his shooting, Anderson nodded. Could be worse, he thought.

'Didn't care for them two fellers as was shot in my place.' Huber frowned, still thinking things over. 'Got a feelin' he done us a good turn with that pair, at least.' He paused, his look questioning as he studied Anderson again. 'Sure you ain't met up with 'em before?'

'Never seen either one in my life,' the dark man told him.

'Uhuh?' This time Huber wasn't too sure. 'They sure didn't take to you, Rankin, an' that's a fact.' Seeing the other man stayed quiet, he shrugged. 'Well, guess I best go 'tend to business. Just let me know when you need the rest of your gear, OK?'

'Thanks, Dutchy. I'll do that.' Anderson shelled out the empties, hearing Huber splash his way back through the puddled mud towards the saloon. He kept the pistol in his right hand for the next try, and this time he hit all five. Anderson nodded, satisfied for the moment. He'd set up the cans and switched the weapon to his left, reloading to shoot again, when a lighter tread sounded in the melting snow behind him. Anderson had begun to turn towards the sound, when he heard her voice.

'You appear to be remarkably proficient with that pistol, Mr Rankin,' Kedron Hemphill said. 'I take it you have had previous experience?'

She stood a couple of paces behind him, hands clasped together as she waited patiently for him to turn around. As he'd expected, Anderson found it was well worth the effort. Kedron was just as beautiful as always, her perfect features matched by that warm welcoming smile that seemed to bathe him in sunlight, the dark gown she wore setting off her pale smooth skin and fiery mane of hair. Meeting those dark eyes of hers, Anderson lowered the pistol, finding a smile of his own.

'Only when I have to, Miss Hemphill,' he told her. 'An' right now I'm a mite out of practice.' He paused, glancing back towards the line of buildings off the main street, whose cleared roofs now gleamed wet in the wintry sunshine, and back to her again. 'Your pa know you're out here, ma'am?'

'Is there any reason why he should, Mr Rankin?' She sounded amused at the question. 'And I'd be obliged if you called me Kedron. We are hardly strangers, after all.'

'My pleasure, Kedron.' Anderson shrugged, awkward under that smiling, dark-eyed gaze. 'Kedron. That'll be a Bible name, right?'

'You are correct, Mr Rankin.' Kedron nodded, the way a schoolteacher might to reward a slow pupil. 'It's the name of a stream in the Old Testament. Father gave us all our names from the Bible. It's something of a family tradition.' She eyed him closely, the smile almost mocking in a pleasant kind of way. 'You think he would disapprove of my being here with you?'

'Well, now.' The dark man scratched at the back of his neck, feeling more awkward yet. 'Just seemed to me, with him havin' no time for guns an' all, he might not be too happy you watchin' a feller shoot off a pistol, if you know what I mean.'

'You would be wrong, Mr Rankin.' For once, her voice reproved him. 'Father may disapprove of firearms, as I do myself, but he has always brought us up to think independently. We live in a free country, and have minds of our own. Father expects us to make our own decisions. All he asks is that we are prepared to abide by the consequences of our actions.'

'An' you decided to follow him into the same line of work, huh?' Curious as he was, Anderson found he couldn't take his eyes off her. Not that he wanted to, anyhow. 'Guess you better call me Josh, by the way. That's for Joshua, reckon he was in the Bible too.'

'Indeed he was.' Kedron laughed, a bright, clear sound like a mountain spring. Anderson decided that it fitted her just fine, like everything else. 'That is a mighty name, a soldier's name. It suits you very well — Joshua.' She studied him once more with that amused smile at her lips. 'You think undertaking is a strange profession for me, perhaps?'

'Well.' Pressed for an answer, he hesitated. 'Maybe just a little.'

'The dead must be buried, Joshua,' Kedron reminded him. 'Someone must do the work. Surely it's an honourable calling, to see our fellow creatures meet their Maker in a decent and dignified way. Even if they lived evil lives, and died by violence, like the men in Huber's saloon.'

'Yeah, Kedron. Reckon you're right, at that.'

'In any case, it's something I've grown up with.' Kedron touched a hand to her red, coppery locks, her look grown thoughtful. 'It was natural I should take an interest. Gilead was already helping Father with the business by the time I came to decide.'

'But Abigail didn't, huh?'

'No.' Something like a shadow passed across her face, and for a moment there was sadness in her voice. 'Like all of us, she made her choice, and must live with the consequences.' She lowered her hand to her side, and shook her head. 'I'd prefer not to discuss my sister. It's a painful subject, you understand.'

'Whatever you say, Kedron.' Anderson was none too sure he did, but he figured he wasn't about to get an explanation.

'I believe you said you intended to travel north.' Suddenly she was bright and self-assured once again, the sadness forgotten. 'I hope you'll pardon my being so inquisitive, Joshua — it's none of my business, I know — but that would mean Canada. Am I right?'

'Sure, Kedron.' He shrugged, trying not to show how she'd thrown him. Anderson had been expecting the question for a while, but not here, and not from her. Somehow, he found it was tougher lying to Kedron than to anyone else. 'No reason why you shouldn't know it, I guess. Friend of mine reckoned he knew where I could find work with a logging company, just over the border. That's where I was headed.'

'A logging company?' Kedron sounded puzzled. Under the scrutiny of those eyes, Anderson began to feel uncomfortable again. 'I imagine that must be a new departure for a man like yourself?'

'Well, it ain't loggin' exactly, Kedron.' The dark man stroked the gunbarrel against his cheek as he answered. 'More standin' guard while the fellers work. I heard tell there was some trouble with outlaws stealin' the timber, somethin' of the kind.'

'I see.' Kedron thought that over for a moment, sober-faced. 'So you intend to call on him, then?'

'Guess so.' It was Anderson's turn to frown. 'Reckon he might not be expectin' me after so long. Tell you the truth, the job could be gone by now, if it was ever there.'

'Yes.' When Kedron frowned, he figured it only made her even prettier. 'You have been delayed here for several days.' She paused for a while, then glanced up to him again, that glorious smile returning. 'Something's just occurred to me, Joshua. Father might be able to offer you work for a time, I'm sure he said something the other day about being shorthanded. Why don't you ask him?'

'Well.' The unease showed plainly in Anderson's face. 'Ain't too sure about that, Kedron.'

'No, Joshua.' Seeing his troubled expression, she shook her head, coming out once more with that bright, springwater laugh of hers. 'Not under-taking, I promise. And only for a time. Go and see him now, he'll explain it to you.'

'I might just do that.' Seemed to Anderson that smile was catching. All he had to do was look at her, and he couldn't help but smile himself. 'Thanks again, Kedron.'

'My pleasure, I do assure you.' Kedron smiled even more brightly, clapped her hands briskly together as business was concluded. 'Well, this has been a most enjoyable conversation, Joshua, but other tasks are waiting. If you will excuse me.'

'Sure, Kedron.' Dazzled by the smile, Anderson fumbled for words. 'Always good to see you, you know that.'

She was already turning away as he spoke, moving light-footed with one hand holding her long skirt clear of the slowly thawing slush. Anderson stood and watched her go, giving her all his attention. It was as if he couldn't see enough of Kedron, even walking away.

He was still following that dark-clad shape as it flitted down the alley between the buildings, when he heard the clink of glass. Shifting his glance towards the sound, he saw Abigail Hemphill outside the back room of Huber's saloon, hoisting a heavy crate of bottles from the ground. From here it was too far to make out the expression on her face, but for a second or so she halted, and he knew she'd seen him. Then the tall woman turned from him, shouldering the door to carry the crate back inside.

Anderson watched the door slam behind her, and shrugged, his look coming back to that row of metal cans. Lifting the Colt left-handed, he triggered a rapid flurry of shots, switching aim smoothly as each bullet was sent. Four cans he plugged cleanly, the last but one escaping with a nicked edge. Anderson shucked and reloaded, frowning thoughtfully as he eased the pistol back into its holster. Concentration was suffering a little, and he reckoned that Kedron and her sister might have something to do with it. Time he went to see Hemphill, and asked about the job.

Abigail came back out from behind the saloon, butting her way through the doorway of the storehouse as he neared the line of buildings on Main Street. Seeing him closer to hand, the sandy-haired woman scowled, bending to lay hold on a second crate.

'Miss Abigail.' Anderson touched the brim of his hat, aiming to walk on. This time, though, it seemed she had other ideas.

'See you been chewin' the fat with Miss High-an'-Mighty Kedron.' Abigail spoke sourly, freckled features clenched into a frown. On him, her pale blue eyes were harder than hammered steel. 'Reckon you must've enjoyed that — Mr Rankin!'

'Reckon you could be right, Miss Abigail.' The dark man nodded, meeting her accusing stare. 'Ain't no business of mine, Miss Abigail, but it seems to me that ain't no way for a young lady to talk about her sister.'

'You're right, Rankin. It ain't no business of yours.' Abigail spoke through tightly set teeth, grasping the crate with its rattling freight of bottles and heaving it from the ground. 'Let's just say the two of us don't always see eye to eye, OK?'

'If you say so, ma'am.' Anderson started in towards her as he answered. 'That'd be on account of you workin' with Dutchy, I guess.' His flint-grey gaze rested with her, questioning. 'How come you didn't want to do that, if you don't mind me askin'?'

'I got my reasons!' Anger flared in her voice, showed in the flush that heated her broad features with their spatter of freckles. 'Told you already to mind your business, feller. Now if you ain't got nothin' else to tell me, I got work to do.'

'You want a hand with that crate, I'd be glad to help.'

'I can manage, thanks.' The sandy-haired woman backed for the door, the crate held firm in her strong-muscled grip. 'Wouldn't take your kind of help anyhow, Rankin.'

'Your choice, Miss Abigail.' Anderson shrugged. 'No skin off my hide, ma'am, but I reckon your sister cares a heap for you, all the same. Wouldn't do no harm to treat her a little kinder.'

Abigail tightened her grip on the crate so hard the bone of her knuckles showed through. For a while Anderson wondered if it was about to come flying his way, bottles and all.

'You don't know a damn thing, Rankin!' Abigail slammed back into the door, shoving it open. The blue eyes blazed at him from a face so hot it looked ready to catch fire. 'Dumb an' crooked both, that's you! Once you're ready to tell it straight, I might just listen. Meantime, get the hell out of my way and stay there, you hear?'

She barged back through the doorway, letting it bang shut behind her. Inside he heard the thunderous crash as she set down the crate. Huber could have some busted bottles there, he thought.

'I hear you, Miss Abigail,' Anderson said.

Only the closed door caught the words, and he guessed it didn't have any answers for him. Anderson swung on his heel, treading muddy slush that spattered his boots. He rounded the corner of the last in the line of buildings, and cut through the alley and on to the street.

On the far side of Main Street, Hemphill's place stood back from the rest, the last of the snow clinging vainly to its shingled roof. Anderson tried the door of the funeral parlour, stepped inside as it creaked stiffly open. A heavy silence met him, soft and smothering as a shroud. It hung over the room with its ranks of coffins like a Frisco fog, seeming to shut out everything else. Anderson felt that stillness press on him so hard it was almost an effort to breathe. Not a sound but for the creak of the door as he entered, and no sign of a living soul. Quiet as the grave, he thought. The bed that Hemphill had loaned him stood at the far end of the room, and he made towards it, walking between the polished caskets, eyeing the carved tombstones that leaned against the walls as he went.

He'd nearly reached the bed when a swift slither of movement cut through the stillness, somewhere behind him. Anderson spun to the sound, right hand going down from habit for the Colt on his right hip. The weapon was palmed and clear of leather but Anderson stood frozen, staring like he'd seen a ghost. From the open coffin behind and to his right a gaunt, black-clad figure rose looming upward, pale hands gripping the varnished wood as it favoured him with a cold, spectral smile.

'You know that firearms are not permitted, Mr Rankin,' the apparition said.

'Hemphill?' The dark man's voice choked, turning hoarse. Anderson swallowed and coughed, returning the gun to its holster. 'Hemphill, you just scared the livin' hell out of me.'

'No blasphemy either, if you please.' Jordan Hemphill frowned, grey brows drawing tightly together above the aquiline face. 'For those whose lives have ended, this room is the starting-point for their journey to a final resting-place. Surely they are entitled to some respect in death, if nowhere else.'

'Sorry about that.' Anderson was still getting over the shock of the other man's sudden appearance. 'Reckon you're right there, Hemphill. Didn't mean no offence.'

'I detest profanity, Mr Rankin.' Hemphill's pale, hawkish face still showed disapproval. He swung one long leg over the edge of the casket, climbing out. Standing to his full, towering height, he overtopped the six-foot Anderson by a head. 'Just as I abhor deadly weapons being drawn in a funeral parlour. We had an agreement, did we not?'

'Uhuh.' The dark man met that hard, piercing stare as best he could. 'Guess it just slipped my mind. What exactly were you doin' in there, Hemphill, if you don't mind me askin'?'

'Not at all.' The neatly moustached mouth quirked in a faint, amused smile. 'From time to time I check the dimensions of the caskets myself. Not all our customers are a standard size, you understand.'

'Yeah, right.' Anderson figured he'd heard enough about caskets for the moment. 'Reckon I'll take my gun back over to Huber's now, if that's OK with you.'

He'd started back, aiming to go by Hemphill for the door, when the upraised hand of the undertaker halted him.

'Just one moment, Mr Rankin.' Jordan Hemphill sounded almost apologetic. The tall man let the same long-fingered hand go higher, smoothing his sleek, pomaded hair as the smile threatened again. 'Excuse the abrupt manner, if you please. It's just that our — guests — deserve the best of treatment, and I'm anxious that standards should be maintained at all times.'

'Sure, Hemphill. No problem with that.' Anderson paused, not sure what was coming next.

'It occurs to me that your talents might be of use to us, Mr Rankin.' The undertaker stroked a smooth-shaven cheek, studying the other man carefully. 'From what I have already seen and heard, you are extremely efficient in the use of firearms, and may be depended upon in a crisis.'

'You got trouble here, Mr Hemphill?' Anderson wanted to know.

'Not at present.' The black-clad figure shook his head, his smile reassuring. 'More a matter of covering eventualities, you might say.' He linked his hands together, examining the fingers closely. 'I seem to remember that you had business further north.'

'That's right.'

'A fortunate coincidence.' Hemphill glanced up sharply, flashed a dazzling smile from the depths of his pale, aquiline face. In some strange way, it brought Kedron to mind. 'A substantial amount of my own business activities are conducted north of the border, in Canada. Are you by any chance still seeking employment?'

'As some kind of gunfighter, you mean?'

'I'd rather you didn't call it that, Mr Rankin.' Hemphill sounded hurt. 'An escort, shall we say, to deter wrongdoers?' He paused, pale eyes probing the man in front of him. 'Tell me, what employment were you hoping to find in Canada, once you arrived?'

'Guard for a loggin' company.' Anderson replied uncomfortably, aware of those eyes upon him. 'Last I heard, they'd been havin' trouble with a bunch of outlaws hittin' the shipments, an' needed some protection.'

'Really?' Hemphill sighed, shaking his head. 'These are lawless times we live in, Mr Rankin. And did this band of desperadoes have a name?'

'Feller runnin' the show is called Theo Magruder.' Anderson studied the undertaker as the words were spoken. 'You ever hear of him?'

'Magruder?' Hemphill frowned, thinking it over. 'Yes, I believe I have heard the name. A desperate man, by all accounts, and one to be avoided.' He shrugged black-garbed shoulders as if shaking off the thought. 'And is this post still open to you?'

'Well, maybe not.' Anderson's glance slid away along the line of coffins as he answered. 'It's been a while since they asked me to be there. Reckon they'll have someone else in mind by now.'

'That answers my earlier question. You are still seeking employment.' Once again the undertaker smiled, self-assured. 'Let me outline my proposal, Mr Rankin. My vocation is to make coffins and tombstones, and my products have found favour north of the border. There are well-to-do clients in Canada who are prepared to pay good money for our work, and we make regular deliveries to them. One such delivery will be due by the end of this week, and Gilead and Kedron will have responsibility for its supervision.'

'So where do I come in?'

'It's Kedron who is my main concern.' For a moment Hemphill lost the smile, his hawkish face grown sombre. 'She is a young lady, after all, and after what you have told me about this band of desperadoes in the area — I'd be grateful if you could travel with her, to ensure her safety.'

'How 'bout Gilead? Didn't you say he was goin' with her?'

'Gilead will have other matters to attend to.' The tall man shook his head, still thoughtful. 'In any case, he lacks your proficiency in this regard. I'm prepared to offer you a hundred dollars for the trip, Mr Rankin. When you return, we can discuss terms for your future employment. What do you say?'

'Sounds good to me, Hemphill.' Anderson scanned the other's face, still curious. 'Still one heck of a way from here to Canada, all the same. You surely ain't sendin' us by wagon train?'

'By no means, Mr Rankin.' Hemphill chuckled, regaining his smile. 'You'll be travelling by rail. A much faster mode of transport, I think you'll find.'

'You mean you got a train out there?' Anderson stared. For a while he looked as shocked as he had been when

Hemphill had emerged from the coffin minutes before. 'Ain't seen no tracks here at Kimball's Point.'

'Nor will you, my friend.' The undertaker patted his shoulder, carefully choosing the left side. 'It's a short distance from town, a few minutes' ride. It's my own private branch line, a personal indulgence of mine, you might say. But with the demand for my work, and the difficulties of transportation, I find it's the best solution.'

'Guess you're right, Hemphill.' Anderson nodded, still impressed. 'Seems to me like business must be good, you layin' on a train an' all.'

'Do we have a deal, Mr Rankin?'

'You bet.' The dark man grinned, reached to shake the long-fingered hand extended to him. 'Sure, Hemphill, count me in.' Releasing his grip, he stood back, still beaming. 'Tell you the truth, Mr Hemphill, it was Kedron who told me to see you in the first place. She reckoned you might have somethin' for me.'

'Did she indeed?' It was Hemphill's turn to be curious. 'And where was this, may I ask?'

'Out back of Huber's place.' Caught out, Anderson reddened uncomfortably. Somehow the thought of Kedron never failed to unsettle him. 'I was takin' some target practice, she come out to watch.'

'I see.' The undertaker stroked his chin, half-frowning. 'Well, she was always a most perceptive child, Mr Rankin, and I'm grateful she suggested this visit to you. I feel it will be beneficial for us both.' He straightened to his full, towering height again, the tight smile returning. 'I believe that concludes our business, Mr Rankin. Just be sure you are here with your weaponry for Friday morning. The delivery leaves at daybreak.'

'I'll do that, Mr Hemphill.' Anderson told him. He started away, threading a path carefully between caskets and tombstones, sidestepping the leaning lids. 'Right now, I'd best get my gun over to Huber's, like I said.'

'Good morning, Mr Rankin.' Hemphill had already turned his back and was bending over one of the empty coffins.

Anderson didn't turn to look, heading along the ranks of pine boxes for the door without a backward glance. So far, things had gone pretty well, he thought. In fact, headed north, and with Kedron too, he reckoned they couldn't be better.

All the same, he breathed a little easier when he reached the door, and stepped outside into the fresh, chill air of morning.

That funeral parlour of Hemphill's was kind of spooky, even in daylight.

7

He ran at headlong speed, floundering through bushes and rotten deadfalls, clambering over the roots of massive, looming trees. Running so fast he could feel the thudding of his heart like a bloody drum against his ribs. Heedless of the pelting rain that struck down through the boughs, the snagging roots, the jagged stumps and the moss that caught his feet and slid them backward. He was running for his life.

Ahead of him a thicket shook, a deer flashing past him into the trees. Seal Caller slithered to a halt, checked for an instant before running on. Their faces were in his mind, the sudden cries of terror and pain as the white men rushed down among them with their guns spitting flame and bringing death to men, women and children. The cries of his people, now silenced for ever.

Seal Caller had been luckier than most. He had eaten too much the night before, and gone out to the woods alone early that morning to ease himself. Returning, he had almost reached the village when the shouting warned him, and he saw the whites launch their terrible downhill charge. From the shelter of a tall cedar-trunk he had watched, helpless, as the People ran from their long-houses into the murderous hail of gunfire that cut them down like grain. Seal Caller groaned, shutting his eyes for a moment as he ran. It made no difference, he could not shut them from his mind. The screams, the fallen bodies that toppled and crawled vainly on the ground to escape their attackers. The blood that lapped and fouled the mud. The shocked, staring faces of those who died. Hard as he tried, their vision had not left him. They were with him, as they always would be, until he joined them in darkness.

Two faces stayed with him longer

than the rest. White River Bird, his woman, and their daughter Little Jay. They had been among the first to die, gunned down as they ran from the long-house. Seal Caller choked as he ran, tears filling his eyes to blind him for an instant. He had seen them drop like felled logs before the bullets of the white men, and had known they were beyond help. Now only memories remained to torment him, of White River Bird's warmth at night under the blanket, the black fan of her outspread hair, the smiling face of their child.

A handful had escaped the killing. Blue Thunderbird Woman and Eagle Wind had run for the woods at the first warning of the attack. Seal Caller had seen perhaps two women and three of the older children reach the shelter of the trees before the onslaught struck. They had been the lucky ones. For those who fled less swiftly, or could not run, there had been no hope. Ploughing his way through a thicket that spattered him with rainwater, Seal Caller shook his head and shuddered. He had seen white men before, but these were terrible, more fearsome than the spirit-masks his People used in their ceremonies. The thought of their blood-red, bearded faces, their pale eyes without colour, snarling like wild beasts as they fired without pity into the People, still turned him sick.

One of them had caught sight of him, before he ran. A dark man whose face was smooth. His head was turned away, and he must have glimpsed the Indian from the corner of his eye, but he had swung round swifter than a wildcat and fired his pistol into the trees. Seal Caller remembered the solid thump of the bullet into the cedar-trunk, the splinters of bark that had flown inches from his head. The second shot had clipped twigs behind him as he broke cover and plunged deeper into the woods. Since then he had been running.

They had not come after him, and no more gunshots had ripped into the trees to find him, but Seal Caller had not stayed to watch. He knew that he must run or die. The bow he had taken with him that morning still hung across his back, the birchbark quiver of arrows thumping his hip with every stride, but to use them would have been to perish like the rest. The life he had known was finished, and would not come back. Only one hope remained, that he and the others who had run would survive, and live to build the People again.

All the same, that past clung to him. Seal Caller wiped off the tears on the back of his hand, but the memory of his woman and child would not leave. They were still in his mind as he scrambled up the mossy, rainswept slope, climbing higher and deeper into the shadow of the tall cedar forest.

*   *   *

'Reckon I see you, right enough,' Lee Sharrock said.

He stood at the edge of the trees, palm braced on the nearest cedar-trunk as he looked out and down. Far below the stricken village lay quiet, the shooting over. Smoke still drifted from the smothered long-house chimney, trailing away as it met the outer air. Sharrock eyed the strewn corpses, the blood that leaked to soak into the sand. Further off, the ocean tide rushed up over the rim of the land and fell slowly back, leaving a pebbled foam behind.

He felt Abe nudge against him, thrusting a wet muzzle into his free hand, and paused to stroke the dog's massive head.

'Easy, boy,' Sharrock murmured. He glanced behind him to where the appaloosa stood hobbled, deeper into the trees, then let his look come back to the village and its dead. The gunfighter frowned, his ebony features twisting in a grimace of disgust. He'd seen the whole thing from up here, and it hadn't been pretty to watch. Sharrock was no angel, he'd killed decent folks in his time, but they'd always been men and able to shoot back. What he'd watched here was a massacre, and Sharrock would just as soon have seen none of it.

The white men who'd done the killing were still down there, and from where he was they looked to be mighty busy. Sharrock watched as a group converged on the totem poles that towered like carved wooden giants above the village. They were toting axes and double-handed saws, and now they set to work, hacking and rasping at the bases of the huge posts, cutting their way deep into the wood. After a while the poles began to shudder and sway, as though they'd been caught in a high wind.

'What in the name of . . . ?' Sharrock frowned, puzzled. He heard the creaking groan as the nearest of the totem poles leaned and sagged over, thundering to the ground. Along the line other posts shivered and plunged downward, men springing hurriedly out of the way as they too crashed to earth. Sharrock watched as the men rushed back, swarming over the felled poles. The noise of busy axes and saws rang out again in the momentary stillness. Now it looked like the dumb sons of bitches were cutting them into pieces. Had they all gone loco, or what?

He shook his head, still frowning. Sharrock was damned if he knew what the hell was going on, but whatever it was, the gunhawks down there figured it was worth killing for. He felt the frown bite deeper, still raking the scene below with his dark, stony eyes. Sharrock thought about what he'd come here to do, and decided he'd picked himself a tough chore, all right. Fifteen gunsels against one was real long odds, even with Abe thrown in as help. Looked like he was due to earn every cent of the money he aimed to collect.

Away behind him the appaloosa stamped and snorted, hauling on its tether-rope. In the moment he heard it, Sharrock felt the bristling of the dog's fur under his hand. Abe growled softly from deep in his throat, swinging his head towards the trees on the right. Tracking the move, Sharrock caught sight of the lone, half-naked figure that stumbled over the crest towards them, lurching to keep its footing on the slippery ground. Seeing him, the big hound broke into angry barking, tugging against the hand that gripped his collar.

'OK, feller. Come ahead,' Lee Sharrock said.

He'd palmed the .44 Remington from leather as the words were spoken, flipping the pistol into his hand and lining it on the newcomer quicker than it took to breathe. The *hombre* had halted once he saw them, hesitating as if about to turn back. Now, seeing the gunbarrel aimed at his chest, he started slowly forward.

'Steady there, Abe,' the gunfighter told the snarling dog. He eased his grip on the collar and Abe sank down, still growling as he eyed the oncoming stranger. Sharrock gestured with the pistol, signalling the man to come forward. 'Over here, feller, an' make it fast.'

He stood with the pistol levelled, waiting as the man came towards him. Sharrock saw the *hombre* was roughly his own height, but thicker-set, with a broad, powerful chest and shoulders. His features, too, were broad, with high cheek-bones, and from under a fringe of raven-black hair, his dark eyes studied Sharrock intently. But for some kind of skin breech-cloth and moccasins the feller was naked, his bronze-coloured body gleaming wet from the rain. He carried a bow and a quiver of arrows, but so far it didn't look as though he was about to try anything foolish, and that had to be good. Given the choice, Sharrock would just as soon not alert the fifteen men in the village by shooting off his gun.

'You know English, feller?' the black man demanded, and the Indian nodded.

'Sure I know English.' In spite of the pistol aimed his way, the *hombre*'s face showed anger, as though he'd just been insulted. 'You think we're savages or something? My People have traded with the white men for years. All of us in the village know . . . '

He halted, swallowing hard as he tried for the words and they didn't come out. White River Bird and Little Jay were in his mind again, and suddenly it was hard to speak. Reading the pain in those dark, coppery features, Sharrock breathed out slowly.

'You're from the village, huh?'

The Indian didn't answer, pain still in his face as he ducked his head.

'I also saw it.' Sharrock told him. His features, too, were sombre. 'It wasn't good to see.'

'You are not with them?' The Indian had found his voice, eyeing Sharrock warily as he spoke. Meeting that look, Sharrock shook his head.

'No,' he told the man at the other end of the gun. 'I am not with them.'

He stepped back, lowering the pistol. Sharrock slid the .44 Remington back into the holster, and held out his hand.

'I vote you an' me be friends, feller,' the gunfighter offered. 'What do you say?'

Seal Caller stood, eyeing the out-stretched hand as though it was about to bite him. For a moment he thought of his woman and child, and the others who had died. But this one had not been there, and seemed different from the killers he had seen. Besides, he too was not a white man. Seal Caller took a step forward, his own hand reaching out.

'Friends,' the Indian murmured.

'That's better. Just fine.' Sharrock's ebony face cracked into a grin as the two clasped hands and shook. 'You got a name, feller?'

'I am Seal Caller.' The other's features showed the unsure hint of a smile.

'Lee Sharrock.' The gunfighter grinned wider, still shaking the other's hand. 'Good to know you, Seal Caller.' He paused, nodding to where the huge dog lay beside him, the last of the growl still rumbling in its throat. 'This here is Abe, horse back there is called Lucky, an' up to now he has been.'

'A good horse.' Seal Caller studied the appaloosa approvingly. He stood back as Sharrock released his hold, his glance shifting warily to the growling dog.

'Don't worry, he ain't gonna hurt you.' Sharrock frowned in thought, reaching to swipe rainwater from his face. 'Like I say, I saw what happened down there. Those men are no friends of mine, Seal Caller. Maybe the two of us can do somethin' about that.'

'My People are dead.' The voice of the Indian was heavy, bitter with loss. 'We cannot bring them back.'

'Yeah.' Sharrock met the other's stricken eyes, nodded soberly. 'I hear you, friend. What I'm sayin' is, if we stay here, sooner or later they're gonna come lookin'. There any more villages out this way, Seal Caller?'

'Three or four.' Seal Caller frowned,

thinking it over. 'None is close.'

'So tell me the nearest, OK?'

'The villages of the Whale and the Otter People are further north, a day's journey.' For the first time, the Indian smiled slyly. 'For a white man, maybe two days.'

'Uhuh.' The gunfighter flipped droplets from the brim of his hat. 'In case you ain't noticed, Seal Caller, I ain't no white man. You reckon these folks are likely to be friendly?'

'When they see me with you,' the Indian told him. 'In three days' time they will be holding a potlatch, one of our winter ceremonies. All the People will be together at the Otter village.'

'Sounds even better.' Sharrock's voice was grim and determined. 'Reckon that's where we'll be headed, Seal Caller. Let's go, friend. Guess the horse kin take us both.'

He led the way to the hobbled appaloosa, Seal Caller matching his stride as Abe loped close behind them both. Loosing his mount from its fastenings, Lee Sharrock decided he felt better than he had in one hell of a while. All the journey north he'd been counting the odds, wondering if the thought of the money had made him take on too much, racking his brains for a way to bring them down.

Maybe Seal Caller was about to solve his problem.

'Mount up, feller.' Lee Sharrock said.

He set foot to the stirrup, hoisting himself across the appaloosa's back, and reached down to help his new-found friend climb up behind him. Rain still spattered through the branches overhead as they moved into the trees, heading further north.

8

Ahead the slope grew steeper, the locomotive wheezing along the uphill grade. Anderson felt the sudden jolt as the wheels hit ties laid over an uneven stretch, throwing him hard on the sill of the window. The same move flung Kedron against him, her body pressing warmly, close to his. The dark man righted himself with an effort, turned an apologetic look her way. Kedron Hemphill smiled back, her dark gaze brighter than sunlight as the closeness of that trim body threatened to set him aflame.

'Pardon me, Kedron.' He had trouble getting out the words, and the way she smiled wasn't helping him any.

'Don't mention it, Joshua.' For a while she stayed close against him, as if in no hurry to move away. Then the redhead settled herself back into her seat, hands clasped across her lap. Anderson turned his attention to the wave of greenery that flowed past the carriage window. Thick masses of spruce and fir ran endlessly on, matching the charge of the snorting locomotive with a strange speed of their own as it hurtled on into the Canadian wilderness.

'British Columbia, Mr Rankin.' Gilead Hemphill's voice had a rich, self-assured sound. He leaned back over the seat in front of them, pride in the palely handsome features. 'We've been doing good business here for a while now, ever since the old man decided to expand the operation further north.'

'So I heard.' Anderson shifted his glance towards the speaker, mildly curious. He figured this was the most that Gilead had ever had to say to him since he arrived at Kimball's Point, so it ought to count for something. He indicated the moving ocean of timber beyond the windows, unconvinced.

'Tell truth, I'm kind of surprised, Gilead. Out there all I kin see is plenty of trees.'

'Yes.' The young man's eyes were on him, probing keenly. Same colour eyes as Kedron, just like the hair and the pale skin, and the handsome looks. Only thing was, Anderson sensed a mite of hardness there that the sister couldn't match. 'Once we arrive there, I believe you will be surprised, Mr Rankin.'

'Yeah.' Anderson met the other's look, his own dark features giving nothing away. 'Could be you're right there, Gilead.'

He stretched in the seat, easing the kinks out of his long, rangy frame. Anderson had to admit this was the most comfortable train he'd ridden in a while. Apart from the engineer and fireman in the cab, he and Kedron and Gilead were the only passengers, unless you counted the coffins and tombstones in the carriages further back. After the close-packed ride north from Coeur d'Alene, this was something close to luxury, he figured. From the seat ahead of him Gilead Hemphill fixed him for a few seconds more with that piercing stare before turning away.

'I'm sure you will, my friend.' The young man's smile was tinged with malice. Gilead got up from his seat, clung to it for support as the locomotive hammered up the last of the rise. 'If the two of you will excuse me, there are some checks I need to make before our arrival.'

He strode off down the aisle between the seats, and out through the door that led to the next carriage. They heard it close softly behind him.

'Don't mind him, Joshua,' Kedron said. 'We've always been close. He's a little jealous, that's all.'

She'd moved closer to him again, her body brushing against his all the way along. Anderson didn't answer, feeling the warmth of her turn him uncomfortable again. In front the locomotive whistle blasted as they topped the rise and plunged downhill. Black smoke billowed back across the window, leaving smutty smears behind and shutting off the flowing woods for an instant. Anderson turned back from the window, and found that smile of hers lying in wait for him. Seemed like he couldn't escape it.

'Guess that brother of yours has to be right,' he told her. 'Business must sure be good, with your old man runnin' a railroad line clear through into Canada an' all.'

She didn't speak, still holding him fast with her smile and those deep dark eyes.

'Can't rightly think why he needs me to ride herd on you, Kedron.' Anderson spoke awkwardly. Seemed to him like the whole of his body was getting hotter by the minute, just looking at her. With an effort he tore his glance free, eyeing the .45–70 carbine and the loaded saddle-bags that lay beside him on the far side of the seat. The Texas saddle he'd left behind at Huber's place. 'No sign of trouble out here, an' you got your brother along. Reckon it's easy money for me, sure enough.'

'One can't be too careful, Joshua,' Kedron told him. Maybe it was his imagination, but it seemed to him that her pale face was warmer and more flushed than before. He was still thinking about it as she raised her hand to touch his face, still smiling. 'For myself, I'm very glad you're here right now.'

Anderson felt the soft, sure touch of her fingers as they rested lightly on his cheek, tracing the furrow of the old scar that made a white groove in the flesh. He reached to tug her hand away, and Kedron caught his wrist, her face close to his as she leaned over him and drew down the blind.

'No talking now, Joshua,' the redhead told him.

She brought her mouth to his, hands clasping his neck to pull him closer. Anderson felt the kiss set him alight like a match to dry scrub, the blood roaring fierce through his veins. His own arms claimed her, hugged her to him as the kiss went on. When he drew back from her at last he was breathing like he'd just quit running a mile.

'No, Joshua.' Kedron looked up at him, her eyes bright, the smile turned catlike and hungry in a moment. 'No stopping now, if you please. It doesn't have to end with kissing, you know.'

Anderson swallowed hard. He could feel the heart battering his ribs faster than a galloping mustang. This was one hell of a note, he thought.

'How about your brother?' The words came from him as a faint, choking sound. At once she silenced him, laying her finger to his lips.

'Forget him, he won't be back for a while.' Kedron's face had grown hot and flushed, eyes gleaming like shards of polished rock. Her voice, too, was hoarse and trembling. 'Now come here, Joshua, and don't pull away.'

She reached for him again, drawing him close. Anderson felt the hunger surge once more as their mouths seized on each other, felt the firm grip of her hand on his wrist as she drew his hand to her breast. Full, womanly warmth answered his touch through the cloth, and for a moment the pounding of blood in his ears drowned even the noise of the train. Then the warning in the back of his mind got through to him, and he hauled away, catching her wrists to hold her clear as she came after him again.

'Kedron.' He struggled to catch his breath, forcing himself to look her in the eye. 'I'm sorry, Kedron, but I don't reckon I kin go through with it. Not here an' now.'

His look rested with that pale, perfect face as he spoke. Watching, Anderson saw the expression of angry disappointment threaten there for an instant. Then it was gone, and Kedron settled back into the seat, hands clasped before her as the flush died from those lovely features.

'As you wish, Joshua,' the redhead

murmured. She stared straight ahead, her face calm and composed, as if nothing had just happened between them.

Anderson leaned back in his seat, breathing hard as he waited for his pulse to steady down. He'd done the right thing, that much was sure. He had a job to do out here, and now more than ever he needed to keep his wits about him. The only trouble was, a woman like Kedron made it mighty difficult.

'Kedron.' The dark man spread his hands, trying to explain. 'Listen, Kedron. It ain't that . . . '

'No need to excuse yourself, Joshua.' She turned to him, favoured him with the faintest of smiles. 'No doubt you think me rather forward and unladylike, but it's not every day one encounters a man like yourself.' Seeing him about to speak, she shook her head, laying a restraining hand on his arm. 'No modesty, please, Joshua. There's something about you that appeals to me greatly. Something mysterious, unexplained almost. I believe that's what draws me to you, more than anything.'

Under the scrutiny of those dark, probing eyes, Anderson stayed quiet, hoping he didn't look as uneasy as he felt. This one was way too sharp, he thought.

'I do not intend to give up on you yet,' Kedron was saying. She looked ahead once more, her brow furrowed in thought. 'Unfortunately, a chance like this may not present itself for a time. I have learned to seize these opportunities, Joshua. You must learn to do the same.'

Anderson watched the hand that lay on his arm move gently from him. He was about to answer when the door burst open behind them, and Gilead came back down the aisle to rejoin them.

'Better get ready, Rankin.' He spoke curtly over his shoulder to Anderson, already heading past towards the door. 'Be there anytime now.'

Out in front the locomotive's whistle screeched and wailed, smoke pothering back across the windows as it began to slow down. Anderson saw the flow of greenery thin out and vanish suddenly, replaced by an open stretch whose perimeter was littered with the low, hacked stumps of trees. Leaning up close to the window, dodging the flying smuts, the dark man saw what looked like a huge timber-framed storehouse, whose outer door was fitted with a massive loading bay. Further on lay a smaller, low-roofed building which he figured to be living-quarters.

The sound of the wheels beat more steadily over the track, and he felt the jolt as the locomotive moved around on to some kind of turntable, the carriages uncoupled and shunted aside on to an adjoining track, while the locomotive was brought around to face back the way it had come. The whole thing slowed, shuddered to a halt with a squeal of brakes. Anderson left the window, hoisting carbine and saddle-bags from the ground. He was out of his seat, shepherding Kedron along the aisle, as Gilead shoved back the door, and a group of men came running to heave a wooden ramp up against the step.

'See you made it, Hemphill,' the first one said. He stood back from the ramp, eyeing the man above him. 'Some of us was beginnin' to wonder if you was gonna show.'

'As you see, Magruder, I'm here.' Gilead's voice was cold. He glanced back to where the coffins waited, impatience in his pale, handsome features. 'I've a good consignment for you, if you'd care to unload it.'

'You bet your life, Hemphill.' Magruder bared yellow teeth in an ugly grin. A big, rawboned, hard-faced man whose ruddy features were fringed by a thick, greying beard, he stood a head taller than the men around him. 'Git up there, fellers! Let's check out that cargo!'

Four or five men scrambled up the ramp and inside the carriage, heading down the aisle. Kedron drew back to let them by, but Anderson wasn't so fast. One *hombre* hit against him and rebounded, turning to glare angrily at him. Met by the dark man's flinty stare he flushed hotly, one hand dropping to the pistol in his belt.

'Somethin' wrong with your eyes, feller?' this one wanted to know.

He was just a kid, fair-haired with plump, smooth features and china-blue eyes that wouldn't have looked out of place on a cherub. The full, pouting mouth and the hardness in those eyes told Anderson a different story. He'd met mean kids like this before.

'No offence, young feller,' Anderson said. He made sure he didn't sound like he meant it.

The kid had turned redder, and was set to say a little more, when the *hombre* next to him laid a hand on his arm, drawing him gently but firmly back.

'Just leave it be, Joey,' the second man told him. He glanced back to where Gilead stood by the door, calling out. 'So who's this, Hemphill?'

'Joshua Rankin.' Gilead didn't sound too pleased at the hold-up of his delivery. 'Pa hired him. He's here as protection for Kedron.'

'Is that right?' The *hombre* had turned back to Anderson, starting to smile. 'Looks like we got nothin' to worry about, huh, fellers?'

He didn't turn around, facing Anderson with the same mocking smile as the others burst into helpless, back-slapping laughter behind him. Anderson found himself studying a dark, slim, smooth-shaven man of medium height, wearing the same drab rig of cord jacket and thick wool trousers as most of his friends. Anderson, though, read the black, polished-stone stare directed his way, saw the .36 Navy Colt that snuggled in the *hombre*'s belt, and knew different. This was one to steer clear of, he thought.

'Just do the best I can, mister,' Anderson murmured.

'Yeah?' Feller eyed him like he was none too sure. 'Maybe you'll make it.'

'Hey, Deacon!' Down by the ramp, big Magruder bellowed like a bull. 'Let's have them goddamn crates unloaded! Ain't got all day, you hear?'

'Whatever you say, Theo.' Deacon didn't sound too worried by the anger in the big man's voice. He spared Anderson another slow, raking stare, the smile turning meaner. 'Just stay careful, Rankin. All right?'

'If you say so, Deacon,' the tall man murmured.

Deacon and Creed had already turned their backs on him, the others following as they moved away to where the coffins waited. Anderson shrugged, letting them go. He hoisted the saddle-bags on to his shoulder, and followed Kedron and Gilead down the ramp and off the train. Hostile eyes met him as he landed, and he turned to meet them. There were maybe a dozen more *hombres* in the huge open stretch they'd made by cutting back the forest and clearing the stumps for maybe a half-mile in both directions. Anderson saw the way they'd edged back and around to encircle him without seeming to move at all, and how they stood now, hands resting on holstered pistols as they eyed him like a lobo pack would a run-down white-tail deer. Anderson's grey, flinty gaze took in the little, leather-faced man in the long blanket coat, the stooping, pock-marked jasper whose hand fondled a knife-haft jutting from its beaded Indian sheath. Whoever these men were, he didn't figure them for coffin salesmen. Not like Hemphill, anyhow, though they might find him plenty of customers.

'This way, Rankin,' Gilead told him. He took Kedron's arm, leading her across the uneven ground towards the storehouse. Beyond them wheels rumbled, and four-horse teams hauled a couple of big Studebaker wagons in through the rutted mud to take up position by the foot of the ramp. Creed and Deacon and the others appeared in the carriage doorway, four of them struggling to tote the first of the coffins off the train.

'Hurry it up!' Theo Magruder bellowed. He swore as one of the gunhawks missed his footing and stumbled, the coffin tilting as the others grabbed hastily to keep it from falling. 'Goddammit, Beard! You have to sleep on the job too?'

The *hombre* handling the near end of the coffin was short and thickset, a knifescar winding a pale streak through the darkness of his face. The look he gave Magruder was meaner than a rattler's bite, but he didn't answer back. Anderson decided that Magruder had to be one scary sonofabitch, to keep this bunch of hard-cases in line.

He stayed watching as the four men hauled the coffin to the waggon, grunting and panting for breath as they heaved it aboard. Eyeing the next group as they hoisted a second casket up to join it, Anderson frowned. He knew the coffins were made from solid, polished oak, but this was the first time he'd seen empty caskets weigh so heavy.

'Rankin!' From behind him Gilead Hemphill's voice bit sharply. 'This way, if you please!'

He stood where he'd halted half-way across the compound, Kedron's arm still firmly linked in his own. Anderson moved to join them as the first loaded wagon rumbled off towards the storehouse, and the second creaked up to take its place. Even as he started forward Magruder came up alongside him, his long stride matching that of the dark man across the thick, tracked mud. From behind them both Anderson sensed the shiver of movement as the other gunmen followed, still watching him like hawks as they spread to enclose him again. Anderson glanced to the hard-faced, bearded man beside him, met a slate-cold stare in return. He kept walking, hearing the soft thump of boots in the mud behind them as Magruder's hardcase pals kept them in sight.

Up ahead of them the wagon had reached the storehouse. Men hurried to shove back the hatch above the loading bay, and the big Studebaker was wheeled back to set down its freight. Gilead and his sister stepped over the last few ruts to join them, Kedron carefully holding the skirt of her long dress clear of the mud. They halted in front of the main storehouse building, whose massive doors were heaved slowly back. Anderson and Magruder caught up with them maybe a couple of minutes later.

'Reckon we got somethin' for you too, Hemphill,' the bearded man said. He turned, favouring Anderson with his yellow, wolfish grin. 'What you think of that, feller?'

Peering inside the storehouse, Anderson found he was too shocked to answer. Right now he felt as though some wild Comanche buck had just whipped him across the head with a stone war-club. The dark man stared at stacks of massive timber hunks that lay piled one on another in the gloom, all of them set with carved faces that glared and snarled right back at him. Faces of wolves and bears, knife-beaked hawks and killer fish, all looking his way. As if somebody had to pay for what had happened to them, and they figured that he was the one to blame.

'Damn good haul, ain't it?' Theo Magruder chuckled, the ugly grin still splitting his bearded face. 'Took us a while to git it down here, an' that's the truth.'

Anderson heard Gilead say something in answer, but it seemed that the shock had left him so numb he couldn't make out the words. What he was looking at turned him sick. It was as though someone had just gutted a church someplace, and piled up busted statues and crucifixes out of sight in the dark. He was still shaking his head, trying to find words of his own, when another louder voice cut through the silence.

'That's him!' Charlie Fairchild yelled. 'That's him, goddammit! He's the feller shot it out with us at Dutchy Huber's place!'

He ducked out around the storehouse door, coming suddenly into sight. Breaking from his trance, Anderson had just enough time to recognize the gaunt figure with its sunken, hollow cheeks and cold pale eyes before that long-barrelled weapon swung towards him. He dived sideways into Magruder, the tall frame of the bearded man shielding him from the gun as the pair of them went down kicking and floundering in the mud. Away beyond them he heard Kedron's high-pitched scream, and the thud of booted feet that came in towards them at a run.

An arm locked around his neck, fighting to drag him over backwards. Anderson fell back quicker than expected, swung an elbow as the grip loosened. Hit in the throat, Magruder choked, reached to catch the dark man's gun-wrist in a bruising hold as Anderson struggled to pull the Colt free of leather. Magruder's ruddy, hard-planed face heaved up in front of him, teeth set in a furious snarl of effort as he clawed his own pistol loose. Anderson ducked as the gun lashed for his head, grimaced as the hard metal hit his shoulder. He drove forward, slamming his skull into the other's bearded face. Theo Magruder managed a muffled, spluttering grunt of pain as hard, unyielding bone smashed into his mouth and nose. He went down heavily, crashing to earth.

Booted feet were all around him, a living forest that hemmed him in as he fought to rise. Through the legs of the gunhawks Anderson saw Kedron turn towards him, struggling and screaming in the firm grasp of her brother as Gilead pulled her away. From here he couldn't make out what she was saying, but he guessed it had to be 'don't hurt him!' And he knew there wasn't a chance they'd do what she asked.

'Damn it, Gilead! Leave her be!' Anderson shouted.

He felt the sickening jolt as the first boot thumped into his ribs, and folded with a gasp of pain. Anderson tried to roll clear, knees and elbows lifted to protect his body as more boots and gun-butts took their turn. He caught a glimpse of the lanky, hollow-featured jasper diving in with that long gun lifted, and gritted his teeth as the gunbarrel cracked painfully on his wrist. Hands seized on him, dragged him struggling up from the ground with both arms pinned back. Somebody grabbed his hair, jerked his head viciously backwards. Another familiar face swam back into view. A ruddy, bearded, rawboned face whose flattened nose pumped blood, and whose mouth spat broken yellow teeth.

'Tough bastard, huh?' Theo Magruder's voice was thick with venom. 'Chew on this, you son of a bitch.'

He swung the pistol, lashing savagely

at the helpless man in front of him. Anderson saw it coming, but there was no way he could move aside. A hard, numbing blow struck the side of his head, and he was falling. The whole world was lost to a thick, heavy shroud that folded itself over him, while he dropped like a stone into deeper darkness.

That was the last thing he remembered.

9

Somewhere overhead, away in the distance, he caught a faint glimmer of light. So far off, he almost didn't see it at all, as though he was stranded at the bottom of a mineshaft, or a deep-sunk well, too far down to climb out. Which was kind of crazy, because he could feel himself drifting up to meet that ghostly light, as if something he couldn't see was hoisting him there. And as he rose, the faces of two women were in his mind.

Anderson saw the flawless looks of Kedron, and Abigail with her blunt, freckled features and tousled sandy hair. One of them was calling out, just like the last time. 'No! No! Not that!' And when he came to think of it, he could have sworn it was Abigail's voice he was hearing.

The light swelled up suddenly, seared

into his eyes to blind him for the moment. Anderson groaned as a vicious, knifing pain threatened to split his head apart, closing his eyes to open them again. Behind the blaze of the kerosene lantern the bruised, bloodied face of Theo Magruder glared down at him, his slaty stare cold and bare of pity. Behind him other faces clustered to take a look. Above them he made out the roof-beams of the darkened storehouse.

'Welcome back, Anderson,' the outlaw boss told him. 'Reckon we was all waitin' on you. Ain't that right, boys?'

He heard the harsh laughter of the other gunhawks, felt the noise ring iron hammers inside his skull. Anderson tried to sit up, bit back a cry of pain as some bastard drove a handspike through the side of his head. Blood crusted on the gash the pistol had made above his brow, and the swelling lump of flesh beneath. They'd roped both hands behind him, the rawhide ties lashed so tight they cut into his wrists.

Another few hours bound like this, and he wouldn't be able to feel a thing.

Not that it was going to matter too much, fixed as he was.

'Who's Anderson?' His voice was hoarse and faint, wheezing like a broken-down old man. That brought a bigger laugh from the gunsels above him, and Anderson winced as the pain struck echoes inside his head.

'Save it, *hombre*.' Magruder scowled. The bearded gang-boss wasn't amused, and it showed. 'No call for you to waste any more of our time, mister. We know who you are, an' why you're here. Only it ain't gonna work, you hear me?'

'Uhuh.' With an effort, Anderson raised his head, taking in the pitiless faces that hemmed him in from above. The quiet, dark-eyed gunhawk they called Deacon stood next to Magruder, still smiling as he studied the prisoner at their feet. Further out came the gaunt, skeletal-faced feller with his long-barrelled gun, then the little leathery-faced oldster and the *hombre* with the scar. The last man on the edge of the bunch he couldn't quite make out, but it didn't look like the blond kid was with them. Or Gilead, or Kedron.

'How'd you git word of that, Magruder, if you don't mind me askin'?'

'We got ways, Anderson.' The gang-boss found his unpleasant grin once more. This time, with the busted teeth, it looked even worse. 'The way this operation's set up, you might say we got eyes an' ears most every place you care to name. We had word of you some while back, before you headed north. All the way here, we've been waitin'.'

'Only up to now, it ain't worked out too well, huh?' Anderson said.

He shifted his glance to the lanky, gaunt-faced gunman, forcing a smile, and drew up his legs against the kick he knew was coming. Skull-face swore as his boot slammed on the bound man's hip, and eased back for another try.

'That's enough, Fairchild!' Magruder's voice cracked like a blacksnake whip, and the gaunt man pulled out of the kick half-way, scowling as he lowered his foot to the ground. Theo Magruder set down the lantern, frowned as he eyed the bound figure in front of him. 'Sure, Anderson, you done all right for a half-breed lawjohn, but it ain't good enough. All you done was cause us a few worries, an' now it don't matter no more.'

'Ask him about his friend, that black sonofabitch,' Charlie Fairchild muttered. He glared down at Anderson as though he couldn't wait to kick him again. 'What happened to that black boy, mister lousy lawman? Where is he?'

He leaned in closer with the words, shoving the gun at Anderson's face. Now the weapon was inches from him, Anderson realized that what Fairchild was toting was an old Colt revolving rifle, whose six chambers and elongated barrel gave it the look of an absurdly long pistol fitted with a carbine stock. Hell of a way to find out, the dark man thought.

'He ain't my friend, *hombre*,' Anderson told Skull-face. He flinched as more pain stabbed through his head as he spoke. 'Don't know where he is, neither.'

'I said ease off, Charlie!' Magruder's voice cut in again, hauling Fairchild back surely as a flung rope. The tall, bearded gunhawk shook his head, arms folded as he eyed the man on the floor. 'We don't need no answers, so save us the hero stuff, OK? An' you, Charlie, shut your mouth. You an' Tevis an' the others did a lousy job, an' you're the one lucky enough to stay breathin'. Best make sure you don't mess up again, understand?'

'I hear you, Theo.' His face sullen, Fairchild looked down at his boots. 'Ain't gonna happen again.'

'It better not,' Magruder told him.

'So what you fellers got in mind for me?' Anderson asked. He figured he knew the answer, and the fresh outburst of laughter told him he'd been right.

'Salty son of a bitch, ain't he?' Joel

Deacon chuckled. His pale face expressed a blend of amusement and grudging admiration. The dark gunhawk stroked the pistol in his belt, raking Anderson over with those black, stony eyes. 'Pity you an' me ain't never met up one to one, Anderson. Sure would be a pleasure to take you on, mister.'

'Another time, maybe.' Anderson held that probing stare as he answered.

'Forget it! There ain't gonna be no other time!' Magruder broke in curtly, cutting them short. The outlaw boss turned on the stumpy oldster, his voice harshening. 'Etheridge, you an' Beard better go help out with the shipment. Plenty of loadin' to be done yet.' He glanced sideways to the still smiling Deacon. 'Joel, you go with 'em. Make sure there ain't no mistakes.'

'You got it, Theo.' Deacon grinned, tipping his hat in a mocking salute to the man on the floor. 'Be seein' you, Anderson. Or maybe not.'

He turned, heading after Etheridge and the scar-faced Beard as they moved out of sight, going deeper into the gloom of the storehouse. Peering past the men nearest to him, Anderson saw figures moving back and forth, carefully loading the carved totem sections inside the empty coffins. So that was how they worked it, he thought.

'Kinda neat, huh?' Magruder grinned contentedly, giving a further glimpse of jagged yellow teeth. The bearded man pointed to two unlidded caskets close by the wall, leaned over one of them to hoist out a couple of clinking burlap sacks. He held them up in front of his prisoner's face, the ugly grin widening. ' 'Course, these two coffins came in weighin' a mite heavier'n the rest. This is what you might call payment for services rendered.'

'Yeah. I get the picture.' Anderson didn't sound like the knowledge made him any happier. 'An' now they'll all weigh pretty much the same, goin' south?'

'Got it in one.' Magruder lowered the sacks back into the casket, stood straight to brush the dust from his hands. 'Trouble is, it ain't about to do you no good, where you're headed.' He beckoned to the gunman furthest from him. 'Ireson, get over here.'

Ireson stepped into the lamplight, and Anderson decided it didn't improve him any. The *hombre* was thin and stooping, with a narrow, pock-marked face. Greasy mouse-coloured hair straggled out from under the brim of his hat, and the close-set eyes were dull and empty of feeling. Now he stood looking down at Anderson, and fondling the haft of his knife in its beaded sheath.

'You an' Fairchild got the job,' Magruder told him. 'Take him out from here to the woods, and get it over with. OK?'

'Could do it right here, boss.' Ireson offered. As he spoke, he gave a look that sent an icewater chill down the back of Anderson's neck. 'Wouldn't be no trouble at all.'

'Not here, Cage.' Magruder shook his head, keeping his ugly 'gator's grin.

'Don't want to upset the little lady now, do we? Reckon she took a shine to you, Anderson. Ain't that right?'

'Where is she?' Remembering Kedron, Anderson leaned forward, wrestling vainly with his bonds. Pain stabbed through his skull, and he dropped back again, feeling the thongs cut into his wrists. 'What the hell have you done with her, you sonofabitch?'

This time he wasn't quick enough, and Magruder's aim was sure. Anderson gasped as the outlaw's boot thudded into his groin to send a fiery agony flooding through him. For a while he huddled, bent over with his face against the dirt, waiting for the worst of the pain to die.

'Don't trouble over her,' Magruder told him. 'She's safe enough.' The tall, rawboned outlaw signalled to Fairchild and Ireson, his voice impatient. 'Get him out of here!'

He stood back as the two men grabbed their captive and hauled him roughly to his feet. Anderson gritted his teeth, still fighting the pain that racked him. He stumbled awkwardly forward, lurching to stand as they held him upright between them, heading for the open doorway. Behind them, Theo Magruder called out again.

'This time do it right, Charlie!' the gang-boss shouted. 'No mistakes, you hear?'

Fairchild muttered a low-voiced answer that Anderson didn't catch. Ireson said nothing, giving a vicious twist to the dark man's arm and dragging it higher up his back. The two of them shoved him out across the open ground, moving around the rear of the store-house and living-quarters to where lopped stumps marked the edge of the woods. From the corner of his eye Anderson glimpsed other gunmen going to and from the storehouse with the loaded coffins, and heard the rumble of wheels as the wagons made their journey to the waiting locomotive, and back again. It would be a while before they were finished, he thought.

Not that he'd be around to see it.

A shove in the back sent him stumbling on, the hacked tree-stumps looming closer. Anderson took a deep breath, fighting the pain and the numbness in his wrists. Looked like he'd run his head into the noose they'd fitted for him. All he could do now was play it through to the finish, and hope that by some miracle he came out ahead.

Trouble was, short of a miracle, he didn't give too much for his chances.

10

Beyond the row of stumps, the forest closed in. Dusk gave way to deeper shadow as tall stands of pine and spruce reared to shut out the light. Anderson went ahead, feet crunching on litter and needles, pausing every once in a while to overstep a decaying deadfall in his path. Behind him he heard their footsteps follow. Maybe a half-hour's walk into the trees, the ground took an uphill slope, fresh stands of timber crowding the crest. He'd started to climb it, struggling against the grade, when the voice of Ireson halted him.

'That's far enough!' Ireson called. He drew the knife, pointed with it to where what looked like a cave made a hollow in the slope. 'Over yonder, lawman!'

Anderson eyed the long-bladed knife, curved like a Bowie blade, and tried not to think too hard about it slicing into his flesh. For a moment he thought about running, but Fairchild was standing close with the Colt rifle levelled on him, and at this range there was no way the gaunt *hombre* was going to miss. Anderson came down the slope, and moved slowly towards the mouth of the cave.

'Oughta do to stow him in, once we're through.' Cage Ireson sounded like he'd begun to enjoy himself. 'OK, Anderson, hold it right there.'

Anderson halted a few yards in front of the cave entrance. Seemed to him some kind of faint but ripe scent wafted from inside the place that hung in his nostrils and made him uneasy in his mind. He didn't have long to think about it. Ireson was right behind him, and the point of his knife pricked the back of Anderson's neck, drawing a slow trickle of blood as it broke the skin.

'Just a little somethin' on account,' the pock-marked *hombre* told him. He chuckled softly, his sour breath fanning Anderson's face. 'No call for us to hurry this, huh, Charlie? Slow or quick, he's just as dead, an' this way we git to have ourselves a little fun. Ain't that right, Mr Anderson?'

He touched the knife to the dark man's earlobe, flicked the weapon in a swift downward stroke. Anderson cried out sharply as the razor-edged blade slashed the flesh, the sudden pain following. Blood ran hot and thick from the wound, spattering his neck and the collar of his coat and shirt. Ireson kicked him hard behind the knee, and he went over, ploughing face down into the litter and debris of the forest floor.

'Don't sing out too loud, lawman.' The gunhawk said. He walked lazily over to where Anderson lay sprawled, wiping the bloody knife on his cord pants. 'Ain't hardly started yet.'

'Somethin' stinks around here, Cage,' Charlie Fairchild said. The gaunt-featured outlaw sniffed the air, thin mouth puckering in distaste, and glanced towards the cave. 'You reckon some critter died in there, maybe?'

'What the hell do I care?' Ireson shrugged, dismissing the other's thought. He crouched beside the fallen man, grabbing lank black hair to drag Anderson's head back, and smiled as he eyed the curved knife he held in the other hand. 'Now here's somethin' should have you singin' like a jaybird, Mr Anderson.'

That heavy, thick scent was in his nostrils again, wafting from the cave. Anderson registered the smell at the back of his mind, as something too distant to count. Ireson's knifeblade slid gently down the front of his shirt, popping buttons and tugging threads on its way for his bruised groin. The dark man tensed himself in readiness for the cut, and Cage Ireson laughed, resting the keen point for a moment above his crotch.

'Take it easy, lawman,' he told Anderson. 'Gonna feel it soon enough.'

'Don't like this place, Cage,' Fairchild muttered. He edged around the two of them, stepping back across the mouth of the cave. He didn't see the fallen branch and its stack of twigs that lay behind him, and when they caught the back of his legs he staggered and almost fell. Fairchild's booted foot smashed through the mass of twigs, and one of them cracked with a noise like a gunshot. Deep inside the cave, something growled and started moving.

'My God, Cage!' Fairchild's voice was shrill with fright. 'What the hell . . . ?'

He had no time to get out any more. A dark, massive, boulderlike shape came from the cave-mouth faster than a cannon-shell, hurtling straight at him. All of a sudden the air was full of that ripe, heavy smell, and his screech drowned to a terrible, deep-throated roar. The last thing Fairchild saw was an enormous paw the size of a barrel-head and sporting a vicious set of claws, swiping at his skull. Then it felt as though a locomotive hit him, travelling at speed, and fiery pain raked his forehead as the huge paw struck. The blow took Charlie Fairchild clean off the ground, and threw him five or six feet into the trees, the rifle flying from his grasp. He landed hard, and stayed where he fell.

Anderson felt the surge of the huge critter plunge past him where he lay on the ground, the ripe stink filling his nostrils until he was ready to choke. The big grizzly paid him no mind, didn't spare a look for Fairchild either. Instead it went charging after the one man who was still moving, and who now ran yelling and howling for his life through the woods beyond.

Cage Ireson had started running the minute his friend called out. As gunhawks went, he ran pretty fast, but Anderson knew he hadn't a hope in hell. Big and clumsy as the grizzly looked, it covered the ground quicker than any running man. Ireson made no more than twenty or thirty yards before it caught up with him, and after that he was out of luck. Anderson saw that paw slam across the pock-marked *hombre*'s back, heard the terrified scream of the outlaw as he hit the ground, and bit down on a foul taste in his mouth. Disregarding the pain and the pouring blood from his gashed ear, he rolled on his back and slithered quickly towards the fallen knife. It seemed to take an age before he got it positioned blade-upwards, but the weapon was honed so keen he had no trouble slicing through his rawhide ties. Anderson yelled with pain as the circulation came back, and got hurriedly to his feet. He grabbed up the Colt rifle that Fairchild had let fall, and took off running hard, heading in the opposite direction away from the cave. He glanced back once as he ran, and saw the bear shaking Cage Ireson like a cloth doll in its jaws. The gunman wasn't yelling any more, hanging loose-limbed and unresisting in the grizzly's hold. Anderson saw the bear throw Ireson down, biting at his head, and heard the crunch as the skull gave way. The dark man halted by a spruce tree to throw up. He leaned there a moment, retching, before running on.

Deep into the forest, stumbling and hitting against tree-trunks and low-hung boughs, Anderson figured he might just be safe when a ferocious snarling broke out from ahead. A huge grey blur of movement hurled itself at him, slammed into his chest to hammer him down in the litter. Anderson snarled back, hands on the thickly furred throat as he fought to hold off a set of snapping jaws from his face. Hell of a way to finish, after getting away from the grizzly, he thought.

'Abe!' The voice cut from further back in the trees, slashing like a whip. 'Down, Abe! Back off, feller! Now!'

At the sound of that voice the massive dog gave back, growling as it went. Anderson let go his grip on the animal's throat and lay still, waiting. No sense his moving now, with the hound still growling low in its throat as it watched him from a couple of feet away. Besides, he'd already recognized the voice.

'Thought I told you to stay clear of me, Anderson,' Lee Sharrock said.

He came forward to take a closer look, leading the appaloosa by its rope. Seeing the figures of man and horse loom above him, Anderson managed a painful smile.

'Said I heard you, Sharrock,' the dark man said. 'Didn't tell you I was about to pay it no mind.'

He saw the stocky, half-clothed figure of the Indian standing alongside Sharrock, and his glance came back to the black man, questioning.

'This is Seal Caller,' Sharrock told him. 'Magruder's bunch hit his village, killed most of of his folks. You could say he's a friend of mine.'

'Good to know you, Seal Caller.' Anderson scrambled up, aware of the dog's close watch on him as he moved. Blood still dripped from the cut earlobe, and he grimaced, holding out

185

his hand to the shorter man. 'Andrew Anderson.'

'Anderson.' Seal Caller shook hands, his face impassive.

'Sure sorry to hear about your people,' Anderson told him.

'Those who did the killing must pay for what they did.' The Indian spoke quietly, but his voice was firm. 'That is the law of our People.'

'Our law too, Seal Caller.' Anderson stood back as the other man released his grip. Glancing to Sharrock, he questioned. 'That'd be for the totem poles, right?'

'How the hell did you know that?' Sharrock eyed him suspiciously, one hand on his holstered gun. For answer, the dark man indicated the gashed ear, and the blood that stained his plaid coat and shirt.

'Just got loose from 'em, ain't I.' Anderson flexed his bruised groin, winced as the pain from his punished body answered. 'Camp ain't no more'n a couple of miles back through the woods yonder, an' I've seen the totems there. Last I saw, they were still loadin' 'em aboard a train that's gonna be bound for Idaho pretty soon.'

'Yeah?' The black gunfighter still didn't sound too sure. 'An' how come you got away so easy?'

'Wouldn't call it easy, Sharrock.' Anderson dabbed at the flowing cut, showed the raw rope-marks on his skinned wrists. 'Two of 'em brung me out to the woods, aimin' to finish me. As it happened, they woke a sleepin' grizzly, an' it took both of 'em down. But for that bear, an' a sharp knife one of 'em left behind, I wouldn't be here right now.'

'You kin tell 'em, sure enough.' Sharrock eyed him warily, still curious. 'An' you say they got a train there?'

'That's right.' Anderson nodded. 'Honest-to-God Pacific locomotive. Rode up here on it myself, figured I might find out more from the inside. Trouble was, they were already waitin' for me once I got there.'

'OK, so maybe I believe you.' Sharrock still looked bewildered. 'But all this killin' for totem poles. What do they aim to do with 'em, once they get 'em back into the States?'

'Ain't too sure yet, Sharrock.' Anderson frowned, uncertain. 'Whatever it is, it has to pay, don't it.' He paused, eyeing the other man carefully before going on. 'Right now they're bein' stowed in coffins for the journey back.'

'Coffins?' Sharrock stared at the dark man as if Anderson had just gone crazy. 'Now I reckon I heard it all!'

'It's the truth. I saw it.' Anderson met the other's disbelieving stare, and shrugged. 'Right now that don't matter. Come to think, you still ain't told me what you're doin' here.'

'I came here for Theo Magruder,' Sharrock said. He touched a hand to the .44 Remington in its holster as he spoke. 'Fifteen-hundred-dollar bounty on him that's good in three states, dead or alive.' He paused, a sudden frown puckering his brow. 'First time I heard it, sounded like good money to me. Since then, I found out how many friends the sonofabitch has out here.' He broke off for a moment, studying Anderson more closely. 'That why you're here? Magruder?'

'Somethin' like that.' Anderson scowled, flicking a bothersome fly from the earlobe that still dripped blood on his collar. 'Looks like we're on the same side here, Sharrock. Best you ought to know Magruder has anything up to twenty men back there, an' three against twenty is long odds, I reckon.'

Sharrock didn't answer, instead glancing to the stocky, bronzed figure beside him.

'Not three only, Anderson,' Seal Caller said. He gestured back through the woods with the bow he held, his broad features set in a grim expression. 'Sharrock and I found more of our people who did not die, and they took word to our cousins the Whale and Otter People, further along the coast. Soon they should be here, and when

189

they come they will be many. Enough for Magruder's men.'

'Seal Caller tells me they were gatherin' for a potlatch at one of the other villages.' Sharrock grinned, glad to be in the know for once. 'In case you ain't heard, that's some kinda ceremony where they sing an' dance an' give out presents. Only once they hear what happened, they'll be along. We were headed to join them on the river when you come runnin'.'

'This is our fight, Anderson,' Seal Caller spoke again, his voice thickening in anger. 'You are friends, and welcome, but this fight is for the People.' He paused, breath heaving in his chest as he struggled to speak again. 'We are not killers, Anderson, we mean harm to no man. Magruder and his men chose us. Now my woman and my daughter lie dead, and many of my friends. Also they have cut down and stolen the sacred totems that honour the spirits of our ancestors. For this, there must be payment!'

He broke off, still breathing hard as he fought to control his feelings. It was a while before Anderson answered.

'Sure, Seal Caller. I hear you,' the dark man said. 'Once your people show up, I reckon we might stand a chance. All the same, we're gonna have to move fast. Once that train is loaded up, it'll be back across the border.'

'Like I said, we were headin' for the river.' Sharrock eyed the battered, blood-splashed figure in front of him, shaking his head. 'Guess we kin git started right away. If you're up to the walk, that is.'

'I'll live,' Anderson told him.

He followed the others as they set off through the trees. Seal Caller led the way, moving with a sure-footed ease through the litter and the fallen brush, flitting shadowlike from the cover of one tall bole to the next. Sharrock fell back to allow Anderson to catch up, and for a while the two of them walked side by side.

'Mighty fine dog you got there,

Sharrock.' Anderson spared a glance for the big, brindled hound that loped silently on the far side of the gunfighter, its head level with its owner's waist. 'Just what the hell is he, anyhow?'

'Abe?' Sharrock grinned, reaching down to pat the furry, bristling back with his free hand, still leading the horse by its rein. 'Irish wolfhound, they call 'em. Got him from a feller come out here from England, worked for him for a while. You might say Abe was his way of sayin' thanks.'

'Why'd you call him Abe?'

'Why you reckon? For Abraham Lincoln.' The black man kept to his grin, ruffled the ears of the hound before straightening up again. 'But for old Abe Lincoln, I might still be sharecroppin' down in Texas. After the war, I got the chance to head north. Least I kin do is name my dog for him.'

'Guess that wouldn't go down too well in Texas, huh?' Anderson had begun to smile.

'The hell I care!' Sharrock chuckled,

glancing up to the horse he led by its rope. 'Might just have called this critter Ulysses S. Grant if Lucky didn't suit him better. So far, I reckon it fits all right.'

'Uhuh.' Anderson eyed the appaloosa, impressed. 'He a present too?'

'Not him.' Sharrock shook his head. 'Won him gambling with a Nez Percé chief on my way up to Coeur d'Alene. Best bet I ever won, better believe it.'

'You didn't have no trouble after, winnin' his horse an' all?'

'No.' Sharrock smiled up at the horse, remembering. 'Nez Percé play it straight, like most Injuns I met. Better'n some folks I could mention.' He looked to Anderson, the smile growing sly. 'Now half-Injun lawmen, reckon that's somethin' else again.'

Ahead of them the woodland took a downward slope, Seal Caller leading along a narrow trail that wound through the trees. Around them the pines thinned and yielded to willow and alder clumps, interspersed with thicker low-lying brush. Far below, Anderson caught sight of moving water, and heard the sound of a fast-flowing current. Seal Caller halted, looking back towards them.

'This is the place,' the Indian told them. He, too, smiled. 'They are here.' He turned, heading down through the willow stands and thick banks of reeds for the river bank. Scrambling to follow him, Anderson saw three enormous wooden dugout boats moored at the waterside, moving slowly to the tug of the current. They were painted and carved with animal and bird symbols, and each one was crammed full with armed Indians. Anderson stared, stunned by the size of the boats. He'd never seen anything like them before.

'Forty feet stem to stern, I reckon.' Sharrock spoke from behind him, halting as the appaloosa baulked at the steep descent. 'Seal Caller tells me they go huntin' whales in 'em, along the coast.'

'Reckon I believe it, too.' Anderson

still stared in disbelief. 'Must be thirty men to a boat there, at least.' Turning, he looked questioningly to the other man. 'Just who are they, Sharrock?'

'We call 'em Haida, that's what he told me.' Sharrock watched as men poured off the dugouts and sprang to land, starting up the bank. 'Guess they got their own name.' Anderson said nothing, watching as the army of Indians flooded ashore. The two who led looked older than the rest, and unlike the half-naked men who followed they were dressed in long feathered cloaks, their heads topped by head-dresses in the form of carved animal masks. Neither man bore weapons, but those behind carried bows and guns, a few were armed only with spears and barbed harpoons. Seal Caller stepped forward to meet them, hand raised in greeting.

'Sure glad they're here, anyhow,' Sharrock muttered, and the dark man nodded.

'Yeah.' Anderson spoke with feeling.

'Now we've got a chance, all right.'

The two of them waited, listening as Seal Caller talked to the two leaders in their own language. Every so often he would point towards them as he spoke. After a while he turned, coming back up the bank, the two cloaked figures following with the other men from the boats. Meeting their unsure stares, the Indian smiled.

'These are One Whale Tooth and Old Otter Hand,' Seal Caller said. He indicated the men beside him. 'They bring the men from the Whale and Otter villages. I have told them that you are friends.'

'That's good to know.' Anderson eyed the two leaders. Both were veterans, their dark faces gullied and seamed with lines, their deep-set eyes black and bright. 'I am Anderson, and this is Sharrock. Mighty pleased to meet you both.'

'Goes for me too,' Sharrock told them.

He waited as Seal Caller and the two

oldsters conversed in Haida. Both men looked his way, nodding in approval.

'I have also told them that you know where the white men have their village,' Seal Caller said. 'They say that if you lead us there, the People will follow.'

'Yeah.' Anderson met the scrutiny of those dark, piercing eyes, touching a hand to his torn earlobe. The bleeding had all but stopped by now, the blood crusting over as it dried. 'Tell them I know this is their fight, but if they will listen, I have a plan. If it works, it may save many lives.'

Waiting for the words to be relayed on to them in Haida, he was startled when one of the elders replied in English.

'We hear you, friend,' Old Otter Hand told him. Seeing the surprise in the other's look, he smiled, his gullied face wrinkling like a leather pouch. 'Among ourselves, we speak the language of the People, but your tongue is known to us. Tell us your plan, we are listening.'

'You got it, chief,' Anderson grinned apologetically. Scanning the broad, high-boned faces that turned his way, he took a breath. 'Well, it ain't much, but this is how it goes.'

He studied those faces as he kept on talking, outlining what he had in mind. Sharrock frowned as though he wasn't too sure, but he caught some approving grins and nods from the listening tribesmen, and figured he had their agreement. Anderson took another breath and went on, knowing he had nothing else to offer them. As things stood, this was the best he could think of, and he knew that if they were to win here, it had to work.

Inwardly, he wondered if it would.

11

He pressed up close to the bole of the pine, feeling the rasp of the bark through his thick plaid shirt. Beyond the last of the trees the camp lay quiet inside its ring of lopped timber stumps. The two Studebaker wagons stood parked beside the storehouse loading-bay, no horses in the traces. A couple of gunhawks stepped out from the doorway, heading slowly across the compound towards the bunkhouse and stables on the far side. Away to the right, the Pacific locomotive sat on its turning circle, the tall chimney puffing as it gradually built up steam. Anderson scanned the open stretch between himself and the storehouse, frowning. From here, it looked one hell of a way, he thought.

'Don't see no guards,' Sharrock muttered. He stood a few feet back into the trees, scowling as he held the fretting horse by its rope. He still wasn't sold on the plan, and all things considered, Anderson didn't blame him.

'Reckon there ain't none, Sharrock.' The dark man eased back into cover as he spoke. 'Magruder an' his bunch have been runnin' things here so long, they figure there ain't nothin' to worry about. Sure ain't countin' on us to turn up with this many fightin' men.' Glancing back to the man behind him, he smiled thinly. 'Oughta make it easier for us, I reckon.'

'Maybe so.' Sharrock eyed the far-off timber buildings, still not convinced. Abe pushed up against him, bristling and sniffing the air, and the bounty hunter reached down to stroke the dog's thick coat. 'Still looks a heck of a ride from here.'

'That's why we need the horse,' Anderson reminded him. 'Ain't gonna find one anyplace else. Magruder's wagon-horses are stabled far side of the storehouse, ain't no way we'll get to them first time.'

'Yeah, I guess.' Sharrock scowled, still far from happy as he glanced to the fidgety appaloosa battling its halter-rope. 'Still ain't too sure about this here plan of yours, Anderson. You get this critter killed, gonna be mighty sore at you.'

'If they shoot me, Sharrock, I reckon I'll be kinda sore myself,' Anderson said.

Glancing to the other man, he forced a smile he didn't altogether feel.

'Listen, feller, it's the one chance we got. Storehouse is nearest to us, an' once we're inside, we kin keep them gunhawks busy around the bunkhouse an' stables. Launch a charge across that open ground, we might as well forget it, I reckon.'

'OK, I hear you.' Sharrock shrugged resignedly. The black gunfighter scowled, studying the buildings in the open ground beyond. 'Looks like we didn't git here any too soon, from the way that locomotive is firin' up steam. Guess they must have them totem poles loaded aboard by now.'

Anderson frowned, not answering. From what he'd already seen, he figured Sharrock had to be right. And that could only be bad news. He stole a look back over his shoulder to where Seal Caller and the first group of Haidas waited. Of the thirty men, no more than five or six carried guns, the others being armed with bows and spears. With the other two bands now moving silently through the far edge of the woods, the weapons were the same. The dark man breathed out, wiping a sweating palm on the leg of his pants. This had better work, he thought.

From away beyond the far side of the clearing, out of sight, came the scream of a jay. The sound shivered through the trees, echoes dying slowly. A minute or so later, from the pine woods nearest the smoking train, they heard an answering call, and Seal Caller stepped forward to join them by the edge of the trees.

'It is time.' The Indian drew a feathered arrow from the quiver on his hip, fitted it to his bow. At his beckoning nod the other Haida warriors moved closer, their weapons at the ready. Meeting the fierce, determined gaze of the warrior, Anderson nodded.

'Let's go, Sharrock,' the dark man said.

The black gunman didn't say a word, but Anderson reckoned he could have written a book with the look on his face. Sharrock set a foot into the stirrup and climbed into the saddle, leaned to offer the other man a hand. Anderson caught hold and hauled himself up behind the horseman, his left arm hooking itself around Sharrock's waist while he hung on to the Colt rifle with his right. At a touch from its rider's heels, the appaloosa broke out from the trees and launched itself across the compound in a headlong gallop. The giant wolfhound left cover in the same moment, hitting the open ground in a loping run.

Mud flew, spraying up from the hoofs of the horse. Anderson felt a wet splotch strike his face, hung tight to Sharrock as the appaloosa surged forward with its double load. Away to the right startled voices yelled, and he caught the stabbing of gunflames from close to the waiting train. Fresh spouts of mud geysered up by the feet of the horse, other shots clawing air past his face with a vicious hornet-whine. Sharrock jabbed heels, the appaloosa quickening to a thundering run as gunshots blasted the silence apart. Barely a second later a high-pitched whooping sounded from the woods behind them, and Seal Caller's band burst out of the trees, pausing to fire their arrows before running forward. From the corner of his eye, Anderson glimpsed the sudden rush as a second group dashed in on the men by the locomotive, firing as they came.

'Goddamn!' Sharrock bellowed as he rode.

From over by the stables two gunhawks came running, hurrying to unship the pistols from their belts as they headed for the storehouse. No shots came from the *hombres* by the train this time, though gunfire cracked and hammered on the right. From the sound of it, those jaspers had their hands full with the Haidas for the moment. Sharrock already had the .44 Remington cocked and ready in his right hand. The black man triggered off a couple of wild reflex shots that ploughed up mud just short of the running pair, and for an instant they slid to a halt. It was no more than a split second, but that was all Sharrock needed. He aimed the appaloosa for the open doorway of the storehouse like a rifleman would line up his sights, swung half-way round for a steadier parting shot as the horse went charging in. The gunmen were coming ahead again, having found their nerve, when the bullet struck. With the slam of the pistol the nearer man clutched at his arm, letting his own gun fall. He turned away, bent double in sudden pain. By then, Anderson was no longer watching them, but peering over Sharrock's shoulder at the dark open mouth of the storehouse doorway, which came flying to meet them.

All of a sudden they were hurtling into darkness that swooped over and around them to shut out the daylight. Anderson felt the hoofs of the appaloosa slither in muddy straw as Sharrock called out 'Whoa!' and drew rein to pull it to a halt. He swung a leg, sliding down the horse's flank to hit the ground. Flame slashed the gloom beyond, a bullet whipping a hand's reach above him to thud into the timber wall. Then Abe dived past him like a flying grey boulder, and Anderson heard the gunhawk yell as the huge dog bowled him off his feet. Scrambling up, hoisting the Colt rifle in search of a target, he saw Sharrock turn the horse like a shadowy centaur in the dark, firing as he made the move. The gunflash lit up the cavernous gloom, and Anderson caught sight of the crouching figure who lurched and ran for the door, the gun still in his hand as he clasped his wounded ribs. Sharrock's second bullet ripped into his back, and the *hombre* dropped face down on the threshold without a sound.

'Close the goddamn door!' the black man yelled. He swung down from the appaloosa, running the animal to the far end of the building and making the halter fast to one of the timber pillars there. Sharrock holstered the Remington, tugged the Sharps carbine from its scabbard. Behind him, Anderson ran for the door, hurrying to heave it shut and drop the heavy wooden bar into place. Not far from the tethered horse, the first gunhawk lay pinned to the ground with Abe's massive paws planted on his chest.

'Mister!' His voice carried to them, pitched high in terror above the snarling of the dog. 'Mister, please, don't let him kill me! For God's sake, mister, call him off!'

Abe's bared teeth came a few inches closer, the breath of the wolfhound warming his face, and the gunman lay back, shutting his eyes. Sharrock didn't waste a look on him, heading across the storehouse to where a makeshift ladder stood propped against a loft that held the one window in the place.

'Just stay quiet, gunhand,' Sharrock told him. 'That way, you might come out alive.' Then, to the dog, 'Watch him, Abe!'

He went up the ladder at a run, making for the window. Down below him, Anderson left the door and went looking for something else. The twin silhouettes of the coffins showed blacker against the dark, and he lunged towards them. Like he'd figured, the money was gone by now, the lids thrown off to reveal the empty caskets, but that wasn't what he aimed to find. Beyond the coffins he made out the smaller outline of his saddle-bags, just where he'd seen them the last time he'd been here. Looked like Magruder's bunch hadn't bothered to open them up yet, and now they wouldn't get the chance.

From the far side of the compound came a clamouring of voices and the noise of gunshots. Anderson heard the answering yells of the Indians, and the whistling flurry of arrows. The showdown had begun, and right now he had no way of telling how it would end. The dark man clawed open the saddle-bags, hurrying to reach inside.

With luck, he could help them out a little, he thought.

He was into the bags, and hauling out the weapons they held, when Sharrock yelled from the loft overhead.

'Hey, Anderson!' The gunfighter shouted. 'Hurry it up, you hear! Those sons of bitches are comin' out!'

Anderson heard the shout, and guessed what it meant. The dark man left the weapons lying untended, moving past the saddle-bags and coffins to where his Winchester carbine still rested up against the wall. Mighty considerate of them, he thought.

'Right with you, Sharrock!' Anderson crossed the storehouse at a run, scrambled awkwardly up the ladder with the Winchester in one hand and the Colt revolving rifle in the other. He joined Sharrock by the window in time to see a sizeable bunch of gunhawks come flooding out from the bunkhouse and stables, guns in their hands. Anderson made out the gaunt figure of Theo Magruder leading them in a rush for Seal Caller's band, all of them firing as they went. The momentum of the charge took them past the loft window, bringing them surely into range of the pair who watched them from above.

'You got it, fellers,' Sharrock murmured. He snuggled the old Sharps against his shoulder, peering intently over the foresight. Anderson didn't stay to watch him, already lining up his target. He pressed the trigger, felt the jolt of the recoil. The blast of the Sharps and the Winchester's vicious crack blended closely one on the other, swift as a thunderclap. One of the nearest gunmen went flipping over backwards as if he'd been slugged with a railroad tie, half-somersaulting to hit the ground. On the far side of Magruder, a thickset jasper lost his pistol and plunged headlong forward, seeming to dive face down into the mud.

'Goddammit to hell!' Sharrock gritted the words. It was Magruder he'd meant to hit. He shifted aim as the curse was sent, but Theo Magruder was too quick for him. The tall gang-boss hurled himself round the corner, taking shelter behind the far wall of the storehouse as the *hombres* with him went hunting cover for themselves. Anderson's second shot was hurried, plugging a hat from the head of the last man to show himself. Sharrock's parting shot caught a running gunhawk in the leg, and the stricken man hollered and went sprawling down. A couple of his friends with more guts than sense broke cover and dragged him back out of sight. Sharrock had drawn a bead on one of them almost as they showed, but Anderson caught his arm, holding him back.

'Leave 'em be, *amigo*,' the dark man told him. 'While they're tendin' to him, we got three of 'em out of the fight.'

'Sure,' the black man answered sourly, eyeing the open stretch where only the two fallen gunmen stayed behind. 'Now the bastards are out of range, an' they know where we're hid!'

He swore again, slithering away from the window and heading back down the ladder. Anderson levelled the Colt rifle and tried a couple of shots. The weapon was unfamiliar to him, and he was pretty sure he didn't hit anyone, but he figured it might keep a few heads down, at least. Still hanging on to both rifles, he came sliding down the ladder to where Sharrock waited.

Outside the war whoops of the

Haidas sounded closer, and with them the cloth-ripping noise of arrows and the yells of hit men. Gunshots hammered in answer, and the whooping war cries faltered, wavering back for a moment. Something hard and heavy crashed into the storehouse door, the timber shaking against its bar from repeated kicks and blows.

'Looks like it's you an' me, Anderson,' Sharrock said. He still didn't sound too happy.

'For now, maybe,' the dark man muttered.

Round the far corner Magruder was shouting something to the other gunmen, something he couldn't hear. Heaves and grunts of effort sounded through the wall, and the creak and rumble of heavy wheels starting to turn. Anderson remembered the Studebaker wagons he'd seen on the way in. He was still trying to figure out what Magruder had in mind when he heard the rasp and flare of a tinder-flint, and caught the acrid scent of woodsmoke. Pretty soon he could see the glare of flames dancing between the gaps in the timbers, and the first smoke began to waft inside. The appaloosa whinnied shrilly, tugging against its rope.

'See that?' Sharrock sounded mightily aggrieved. The look he gave Anderson didn't have too much charity in it, either. 'Now they're gonna burn us out! This has worked out real good, ain't it?'

He broke off, coughing as the smoke hit his lungs. Anderson choked as he swallowed his share, hawked and spat before answering.

'Try savin' your breath, Sharrock,' he told the bounty hunter. 'Gonna need it later. 'Sides, we ain't finished yet.'

He set the carbine and rifle down, and bent hurriedly over the saddlebags.

'Sonofabitch!' Theo Magruder said.

He pressed up close to the storehouse wall, feeling the rough-hewn timbers rasp against his back as he hefted the American Arms in the hope of a shot. Magruder's gaunt, bearded face was clenched tight as a fist, his pale eyes savage in thwarted anger. He might have known things were going to hell in a handbasket. Ever since that dumb bastard Fairchild had come staggering in without his gun and with his scalp clawed half-way off his head, whining about Anderson getting loose and Ireson mashed up by a grizzly in the woods, he should have seen it coming. At the time Magruder had been sore enough to bawl Fairchild out before he was led away for them to sew him up the best way they could, but he'd figured Anderson was only one man, and too busy running for his life to cause more trouble. Now, it looked like he'd been wrong.

Beyond him the pistols and shotguns of the men he'd led out boomed and roared, leaden slugs tearing into the oncoming bunch of Indians. A few men fell, and the rest gave back for a distance, leaving the gunmen to encircle the storehouse and the *hombres* inside.

'Get that goddamn fire-wagon in here!' Magruder yelled.

He edged back, watching as big Jeb Callander and five other gunhawks heaved the Studebaker forward at the door. They'd crammed the wagon high with wood hunks and brush from the trash pile behind the storehouse, and now the wind fanned the flames to a roaring blaze. Magruder heard the crash as the Studebaker slammed into the door and sent it shuddering back on its wooden bar. No way they'd hold out for long, he thought.

Flames licked up against the shaking door, the timber bubbling sap and charring as the fire caught hold. Smoke palled black and high, billowing into the storehouse. Magruder heard the squeals of a frightened horse, and the racking coughs of men running short of air. The tall, rawboned outlaw smiled unpleasantly, cradling the shotgun. How the hell Anderson had teamed up with the other *hombre* so soon he had no way of telling, let alone how the sonofabitch had raised a war-band of Indians to come calling with him.

One thing Magruder knew, it wasn't about to do him any good.

The six-man charge drove in again, the wagon with its blazing freight smashing into the door. He heard the bar crack across like a green stick to the impact, and the storehouse door creaked and sagged back, falling open as the fire-wagon drove inside.

'Let's go, boys!' Theo Magruder called. He lunged in through the billowing smoke, eyes narrowed against the heat, eager for a target as the rest of the bunch surged in behind him.

This time the half-breed bastard had run out of luck.

'You see one of these before?' Anderson asked. He drew the bulky-looking weapon from the saddle-bags, his voice hoarse already from the smoke that filled the storehouse. 'Le Mat, they call 'em, shotgun an' pistol all in one.'

'How'd you come by that?' Sharrock

peered at the gun with watering eyes. In spite of the hole he and Anderson were in, he managed to sound impressed. From outside came a battering impact, and the door groaned, threatening to give way.

'Feller I met once. He ain't gonna need it.' Anderson's eyes, too, were red and streaming, voice barely audible as he wheezed for breath. 'Just take it, OK. Oughta come in handy, I reckon.'

He waited long enough for Sharrock to grab the overweight pistol with its single underslung smoothbore barrel, hurried to pick up a .44 Remington from the saddle-bags. Anderson had the single action Army out of leather, facing the doorway with a pistol in each hand as the wagon-ram slammed in again. The door folded and dropped with a squealing, splintering crash like the end of the world, and for the next few seconds he couldn't see at all, the storehouse drowning in a pothering torrent of smoke and flame as the wagon came booming in.

Flying sparks struck his face, hung and smouldered in his hair. Anderson forgot them for the moment, blinking through tear-blurred eyes as he fought to breathe. Shadowy figures loomed through the murk, the roar of the flames muffling the bellow of voices and the heavy concussion of gunshots. One, taller than the rest, had to be Magruder. Anderson read the stabbing tongues of gunflames, fired into the telltale licks of light as they showed and vanished. One of the oncoming gun-hawks lurched sideways, dropping his gun, and took one unsteady step before toppling down.

A bullet clipped the dark man's collar, singed the hair on his neck before embedding itself in the wall. A brief gust of wind blew the smoke aside, and for an instant he glimpsed the crowd of gunmen filling the room. Magruder's tall, rawboned figure was at their head, the American Arms lifting for the shot. Behind and around him Anderson saw other familiar faces.

Etheridge, the little oldster, scarfaced Beard, and the big, bearded *hombre* they called Callander. Then Sharrock pulled the trigger on the LeMat.

With the numbing boom of the explosion Theo Magruder went flying backwards, buckshot tearing a fan-shaped pattern of bloody holes through him at waist height. The gang-boss hauled trigger on his own weapon as the impact hurled him off the ground and into the doorframe, the American Arms blasting wild into the roof overhead. The charge from the LeMat smashed the life out of him, and Magruder died as he hit the doorpost, sliding like a sack to the ground. Beside him a second gunhand yelled and grabbed his arm as more buckshot struck him, pitching over on the storehouse floor.

More bullets were coming back at them, whining and zipping in the smoke-filled room. Anderson felt a shot sear the back of his hand like a branding iron, another slug ruffling his hair in passing. He and Sharrock fired steadily into the murk, but by now he knew they hadn't a hope. There were too many for the pair of them to fight off, and he guessed that pretty soon he and Sharrock were going to die. Maybe there were worse ways. Right now, though, he couldn't think of any.

Jeb Callander broke suddenly out of the fanning smoke, coming at him from the right. Anderson saw the grin on the bearded face and swung the Remington towards it, knowing as he did so that he wouldn't make it. Callander had him targeted when a low, whipping thump tore the air from outside, and the big man froze up stiffly as though he'd been turned to stone. Jeb Callander let the gun spill unfired, his eyes staring straight ahead. He went down heavy as a felled cedar, shaking the ground, the long-stemmed arrow trembling in his back.

Now the air was loud with a high-pitched whooping, and the hiss and thud of arrows. The deadly volley mowed into the gunhawks the way hail hits a cornfield, cutting them down. Anderson saw Hiram Beard clutch wide-eyed at a shaft that jutted feathers and bloody snout from either side of his neck before dropping to kick out his last seconds in the muddy dirt. Cal Etheridge yelped like a kicked dog, reeled back into the wall with an arrow driven through his shoulder. The oldster gritted his teeth, reaching to snap the shaft. He sagged against the timbers, breathing hard as the gunmen who lived hurried to throw their weapons to the ground.

'Anderson!' The dark man recognized Seal Caller's voice. The Haida appeared in the doorway, peering inside as other Indians dragged the blazing Studebaker into the compound. 'Sharrock! Are you all right?'

'We'll live, Seal Caller!' Anderson felt the words tear his chest like a blade as he answered. The dark man staggered for the door, breath rasping in his lungs. Behind him Sharrock ran to free the appaloosa, and Abe left the fallen prisoner, trotting after man and horse into the welcome air.

Outside the compound swarmed with Haida warriors, fresh arrows notched to their bows. It looked like all three groups had converged to take down the gunhawks at the storehouse. Now they herded the survivors together against the charred timber wall, eager for the chance to shoot some more. Anderson counted eight gunmen still living, most with arrow wounds. Old Etheridge was one, and beside him the gaunt figure of Charlie Fairchild sat slumped and sullen-faced, the bloody stitched-up gash in his scalp a reminder of his run-in with the grizzly. They were the lucky ones. Maybe fifteen dead lay sprawled and arrow-stuck in the store-house doorway. The dark man leaned on the doorpost, still heaving for breath. He guessed the plan had worked, but it had been a mighty close call.

'Thanks, Seal Caller,' he told the

grinning Haida warrior. 'But for you, we'd be goners now.'

'You helped us here, Anderson. You and Sharrock.' Seal Caller indicated the bodies, the glowering prisoners. 'You brought them here, and held them for us. Your word was good, you saved lives. Because of this, many of our People did not die.'

Anderson scanned the compound, spitting out the foul smoke-taste. He saw five Haidas on the ground, and others carrying wounds. Still too damn many, he thought. His glance shifted to the silent, outflung body of Theo Magruder, and from there to the man behind him.

'Looks like you got your fifteen hundred, Sharrock,' Anderson said, and the bounty hunter nodded.

'Reckon so.' Sharrock sounded thoughtful. For the first time he cracked a wry grin. 'Figure we did all right back there, Anderson. For a lawman, you ain't so bad.'

'Ain't fixin' to try it again,' Anderson

began. He broke off suddenly, swearing under his breath. Across the compound the locomotive had raised steam, and was already moving away along the track, heading for the woods. Only a handful of Haidas had stayed back while the others had joined the battle. Now they ran vainly in pursuit, their arrows clanking uselessly off the loco-motive body and the walls of the cars.

'No way they're gonna catch up,' Sharrock muttered. He glared bitterly at the moving train, already close to the compound rim. 'Looks like we lost 'em, Anderson.'

'Not yet.' The dark man shook his head. He reached out suddenly, snatch-ing the appaloosa's rein from Sharrock's hand. 'I need a loan of your horse, Sharrock. Guess you an' Seal Caller an' the chiefs will have to run this show for a while.'

'Hey, what the hell . . . ?' Sharrock rounded on him, anger and bewilder-ment in his face. Seeing Anderson's grim, determined expression he shrugged, letting the other man by. 'OK, feller. Have it your way.'

'The spirit markers?' Seal Caller asked. Setting his foot to the stirrup, Anderson nodded.

'On the train, Seal Caller.' He hurried to mount, nudging the horse forward. 'You'll get 'em back, an' that's a promise.'

He shook out the rein, giving the animal its head. After the gunplay and the scare of the fire-wagon, the appaloosa was still spooked, pitching and hauling against the rein, but he managed to get it moving. The big horse cantered and went smoothly into a full gallop as the locomotive reached the edge of the trees. Before long it had begun to catch up with the last of the cars.

The locomotive was travelling at speed now, snorting like an iron monster as it threw smoke and flying sparks backwards over its shoulder. Anderson urged the horse forward, hitting a breakneck lick between the pine trunks. He came up alongside the last car, grabbed the frame of a window. The dark man kicked free of the horse, clung on to haul himself up and on to the roof. Heaving down with both feet, he shoved down the window and slid inside. Last he saw of the appaloosa, it was slowing down as the train ran on. He figured it knew its way home.

Anderson slid down the wall, hitting the floor of the carriage with a crash that shook the breath from his body. He had the Colt up and levelled the moment he landed, but from here the car looked to be empty but for loaded coffins. Whoever was aboard had to be further up ahead. Anderson glanced at the window, where pine boughs flicked past in a blur of motion. Too fast for fancy tricks, that was for sure. Even if he got to the engineer and fireman, he'd be lucky to stop the train. And right now he had no way of telling how many he was up against.

Then again, maybe he had a better idea.

He holstered the Colt, bracing himself to edge over to the nearest of the coffins. From what he could see, it didn't look to be screwed down too tight.

He drew the hunting knife from its sheath, and set to work.

12

He felt the sudden jerk as they halted, the forward surge that took them in through the doorway. Crossing the threshold one of the bearers staggered, and he heard a voice swear as the lid shifted slightly above him.

'Who the hell did this job?' The bearer wanted to know. 'Goddamn lid's half-way off already!'

'Quit worryin',' another voice reassured him. 'We're here, ain't we. Gonna be open soon enough.'

Anderson lay quiet in the darkness, hand resting on his gun. Shrouding gloom enclosed him, pressing down so heavily it was an effort to breathe. Maybe this was the way it would be for him when it really ended, he thought. Right now he couldn't wait to get out of here, no matter what was waiting.

They carried him maybe a dozen

paces, and set him down. Anderson lay still, hearing the thud of their booted feet die away across the threshold. From what he'd heard, he must be in one of the last coffins they'd unloaded. No need for him to ask where he was now, either. All the long train journey back across the border, and the final haul in the wagon, he'd known where it would end. And now maybe he could do something about it.

He waited out a long, echoing silence until the quiet set his eardrums thumping. Anderson took a slow breath, and eased back the coffin lid, heaving it away to the side. It slid away from him quicker than he'd intended, and he grimaced as the polished mahogany thudded against the ground. Anderson scrambled out of the coffin in a hurry, the .45 Colt pistol held out ahead as he searched for a target. He was inside the funeral parlour, just as he'd expected, the ranks of coffins and tombstones keeping silent company around him. He'd begun to relax slightly when a faint creak sounded from the side door to his right, and he swung towards it as the door eased open. Abigail Hemphill entered the room, stood for an instant staring into the levelled muzzle of the gun.

'Miss Abigail?' Eyeing the tall, sandy-haired female, Anderson lowered the pistol. The dark man frowned, puzzled. 'What the — what are you doin' here?'

From the white, deathly pallor of her face, he must have scared her just as much. It was a few seconds at least before she answered.

'I should not be here at all, Mr Anderson,' Abigail told him. She stole a glance at the empty coffin, the other closed caskets that surrounded it, as if expecting other ghosts to rise out of them. 'I came into the parlour the back way, while the place was empty. When I saw the lid move, I hid in the next room, until I saw who it was.'

'Yeah. That I kin understand.' Anderson spoke more gently. 'Don't worry, I ain't a ghost. So why did you come in the funeral parlour anyhow?'

'I saw the coffins arriving.' Abigail's hard-planed features betrayed the worry she felt. 'I've seen them come in and out here before, the same coffins as always.' She paused, her look almost begging as it rested on him. 'That shouldn't happen, Mr Anderson. If they were being used for a proper purpose, they wouldn't be coming back.'

'That's right.' Anderson's face, too, was grim. 'They wouldn't.'

'This time I had to know why.' Abigail's voice trembled, and for a moment she closed her eyes. 'I think I've suspected for a long time, Mr Anderson, but all the while I've wanted not to believe it. Even now.'

'Reckon you'd better believe it, Miss Abigail.' Anderson glanced to the entrance door of the parlour, alert for any other signs of life. 'Tell me somethin', will you? When I was comin' round here, after the ruckus in the saloon, you saved my life. That right?'

She didn't answer him, but her trapped expression told him it was true.

'That'd be from Kedron, huh?' The dark man asked. Meeting his gaze uneasily, she nodded.

'Just who are you, Mr Anderson?' Abigail wanted to know.

'You got the name right,' the dark man said. 'Andrew Anderson, I'm a town marshal in Old Mexico, you might say I was hired for this job. Now it looks like I'm here to give your folks a surprise.'

'You won't hurt them?' She seized his hand, her voice pleading. 'They've done wrong, I know, but they're family all the same. Please don't hurt them.'

Anderson winced as her grip caught the unhealed bullet-graze on the back of his hand, forced himself to smile reassuringly.

'Not unless I have to.' Anderson took her hand and removed it gently from his. 'Miss Abigail, you've done me a big favour once already, an' I'm mighty grateful for it. Gonna ask you to do me another now. Go find Dutchy Huber an' anybody else you kin trust, an' get 'em over here with their guns as fast as they kin make it.' Seeing the reluctance in her face, he sighed. 'That way, we might get through this without any gunplay. OK?'

'If you say so, Mr Anderson.' Abigail fixed him with a final, beseeching look. 'Don't you harm them, mind.'

'Just do it, Abigail,' Anderson said.

He watched as she ducked back through the door, heard it close quietly behind her. From the entrance came the sound of other voices, and he scrambled back inside the coffin, hauling the lid across to cover him. Soon those voices came closer.

'A pity about the Canadian operation,' Jordan Hemphill was saying. Right now, he didn't seem too displeased. 'Room for more development there, I felt. No matter, children, you have returned safely with the shipment, and we appear to have everything we need.'

Anderson heard Gilead's voice murmur something he couldn't quite catch, and Jordan Hemphill chuckled softly.

'That's right, my boy,' the undertaker replied. 'I think we can say that, in spite of everything, business has been very satisfactorily concluded.'

Above him the warm darkness grew oppressive. Time to move, Anderson decided. He pushed back the coffin lid a second time, sitting up inside the casket. Kedron saw him first, and from her shocked expression he wondered for a moment if she was about to faint away. Face blanched whiter than a corpse, the redhead fought to speak and choked on her words, pointing a shaking finger at the man who had grown suddenly out of the coffin, and now sat aiming a .45 single action Army in their direction.

'Joshua!' One word broke from her. A faint, hollow, croaking sound.

'That's right, Kedron,' Anderson told her. 'It's me. Only I ain't dead yet.'

Getting up and out of the casket, he used his left hand to tug the Remington from his belt, levelled both weapons on the startled trio. Father and son might not be as shocked as Kedron, but both looked pretty unpleasantly surprised, all the same.

'One thing you got right, anyhow,' Anderson eyed the tall, black-clad figure coldly as he spoke. 'You're finished north of the border. Magruder's dead, an' most of his gunhawks with him. Now I reckon it's your turn.'

'You appear very knowledgeable, Mr Rankin.' Hemphill seemed to grow even taller, his shadow looming huge on the wall of the parlour as he probed Anderson with those piercing eyes. 'Perhaps you'd care to enlighten us?'

'I know what kind of game you been runnin', Hemphill,' the dark man told him. 'An' the name's Anderson, not Rankin. That's somethin' you an' Kedron have known for a while too, I reckon. US government hired me to check up on a smugglin' racket into

Canada from someplace here in Idaho.' He eyed the smiling, sombre-garbed figure, his voice thickening in contempt. 'Reckon what I found was a whole lot worse. Stealin' totems from Indian villages, an' shippin' 'em back in your coffins. It don't come much lower, Hemphill. Where in hell do you sell 'em, anyhow?'

'No shortage of places, Anderson.' Jordan Hemphill tucked his hands into the pockets of his tailored vest, smiling easily. Of the three, he seemed least fazed by the pistols pointing his way. 'You'd be surprised at the prices some of our richer collectors will pay for primitive items of this kind. Texan cattlemen, oil barons, millionaire industrialists in Chicago and New York. We also do excellent business in Old Mexico, you'll be pleased to hear.' He smiled again, mockery in his voice. 'For this kind of customer, money is no object.'

'Uhuh.' Anderson nodded grimly. 'An' the payment for Magruder went north in the coffins, before they came back with the totems.'

'You are, of course, correct.' Hemphill sounded amused. 'Naturally, the money was raised from other robberies in Idaho and elsewhere, by other organizations under my control. As you may have guessed, Canada was only a small part of my operations, and Magruder one of several — business associates, shall we call them?'

'Sure, an' where better to run the whole crooked deal than a respectable funeral parlour in the Idaho Panhandle!' The dark man couldn't hide his disgust. 'Know what I'd call these business associates of yours, Hemphill, but I got to say you're a damn sight worse.' He paused, looking to Kedron, who now glared back defiantly. 'You too, Kedron. Hemphill an' Gilead here I guess I knew from the first, but I figured you were better. All the way along I've been hopin' you had no part in it. Looks like I was wrong, don't it?'

'Believe it or not, I had hoped for

better from you, Mr Anderson.' The redhead met his gaze unflinchingly, those perfect features unrepentant. 'For a time it seemed you were a man of action, to be admired. Now it's plain you are nothing more than a government hireling, using deceit to worm your way into my father's confidence.'

For a moment Anderson had trouble speaking, shocked by the brazen answer. How in hell could she think she was so right, and yet be so wrong, he wondered.

'You got gall, an' no mistake,' he told her. 'It was you tried to smother me right here, when I was still out of my head after the saloon fight. Thought I dreamed that, but I guess it was true enough, an' but for your sister you'd have made it work, too.'

Kedron didn't answer, watching him with brown, burning eyes.

'Before that I had the two gunhawks layin' for me at Riggott station,' Anderson began. At once Jordan Hemphill waved a hand dismissively.

'My decision, Mr Anderson.' The undertaker sounded like he'd already tired of the conversation. 'My spies brought word of a government agent on the train to Riggott, and Croft and Freeman were sent to eliminate you. In case they failed, Tevis and the others were detailed to ambush you in the woods.' Hemphill frowned, studying his long, polished fingernails. 'Unfortunately your friend Sharrock helped to foil my plans in that regard.' He paused, his glance touching questioningly on the other man. 'I see you do not deny him as a friend.'

'Not any more, I don't,' Anderson said.

'Once these efforts, and Kedron's impromptu attempt had failed, it seemed wise to hire you for the journey north,' the undertaker informed him. 'I had hoped that out there, in the remote wilds of Canada, Magruder would dispose of you with few questions asked. Sadly, he also proved less effective than might have been expected.'

'Why the hell did you do it, Hemphill?' Anderson still had trouble believing what he'd found, and it showed in his voice. 'A man like you. All that Biblenamin' an' teetotallin' an' no swearin' an' stuff. An' it's you sends killers out to murder women an' kids in Indian villages. Not only that, you cut down their sacred totems and cut 'em up to sell to your lousy customers!' He shook his head, eyeing the tall, sombrely coated figure as if Hemphill had crawled out from under a rock. 'Might just as well have bust into a church an' hauled off the altar-cloths an' ripped the crucifix off the wall! How kin a man like you do somethin' that low?'

'You lack understanding, Anderson.' For the first time, the taller man's voice betrayed impatience. Hemphill's cold stare rested on his captor, almost pityingly. 'God gives us talents, and it is our task to nurture and fulfil them. The gift I received was to make and increase my wealth, by whatever means, as five

241

talents were made into ten in the Scriptures. It is he who hides his one talent in the ground who disobeys, and must be punished.' Glancing to the young man and woman beside him, he smiled contentedly. 'Gilead and Kedron understand this. They think as I do.'

'But Abigail didn't, huh?' Anderson demanded.

'I would prefer it if you did not mention her name, Mr Anderson.' In a moment the smile had vanished. 'My elder daughter is a painful subject to us all.'

'That I kin believe.' Anderson's voice grated. 'Ain't hard to see why she took up with Dutchy Huber, neither. Workin' in a saloon is a way more honest than what we got here, Hemphill. I ain't no Bible-reader, but you sure know how to twist the words around so it suits you best. Well, thanks to you there are decent folk lyin' dead north of the border, an' I aim to see you pay for that.'

'I must say, I'm beginning to weary

of this conversation, Mr Anderson,' Jordan Hemphill said. 'Time it was over, I think.'

He nodded towards the door that lay off the room to the left, the opposite direction from where Abigail had appeared. Following his look, Anderson saw the door swing back, to show why the undertaker had been so unperturbed. Two men filled the doorway, pistols in their hands. Joel Deacon, and the blond, moon-faced kid they called Joey Creed.

'Drop the guns, Anderson!' Deacon ordered. His bird-black stare fixed on the lawman, hard and merciless. 'Back up to the wall, an' make it fast!'

Anderson stumbled back a pace, raising his hands with the guns still held in them. A corner of the coffin hit the back of his left leg, jarring the old wound, and a spasm of pain shot through him. Anderson went over backwards to land seated in the casket, still gripping both pistols, as the first shots from the killers zipped viciously through the air above his head. On his other side Hemphill and his offspring scattered for cover, the two men digging hurriedly in the pockets of their coats as the noise of gunshots blasted round the room.

The .44 Remington went off as he landed, his thumb slipping off the hammer. Anderson felt the heavy pistol kick back against his palm, and knew he had no control over what it was about to hit. Joey Creed screamed shrilly like a woman in labour, clutched vainly at his leg as the Remington slug smashed the limb out from under him. The blond kid crashed to the floor, face twisted in pain as he fought to lift his twin ebony-butted pistols for another try.

Deacon was tougher, as Anderson had figured he might be. The dark, pale-faced gunhawk shifted aim swift as a rattler, pressing the trigger on the .36 Navy as he made the move. Anderson heard the bullet rip into the wood of the casket, felt the stinging pain as mahogany splinters sprayed the side of his face. Deacon was fast enough for one more shot that burned a white-hot track along the tip of the lawman's shoulder. Then Anderson had the Colt levelled on him, the foresight of the pistol splitting the gunman's chest in the moment he fired. The force of the .45 slug sledge-hammered Joel Deacon back from the door, reeling against the wall as he hit and lurched forward. The gunhawk coughed, blood spilling from his mouth and staining the front of the starched shirt like an ugly crimson blossom. Deacon struggled to raise the pistol he held, and Anderson shot him again. The second bullet battered him sideways into the wall, and Joel Deacon collapsed, face down, the .36 Navy clattering away across the polished floor.

From the corner of his eye Anderson caught the flicker of movement as Gilead Hemphill lunged in from the side, a short-barrelled derringer swinging up in the grip of his hand. His sudden dash took him across Creed's line of fire as the kid opened up again from the ground. Shots from the plated twin Colts crashed into his body, tore through his chest to destroy the heart and lungs. The impact pitched Gilead across the funeral parlour, leaving a blood-smeared trail as he rolled and came to rest, his eyes staring upward. The hideout dropped from his hand, unfired.

'Gilead!' Kedron's scream put Anderson in mind of a wounded cougar. Jordan Hemphill yelled in the same moment, a bellowing animal cry of pain and loss. Joey Creed swore and slewed painfully around, fighting to get Anderson into his sights. He'd almost made it when the ear-splitting boom of a shotgun blasted the momentary quiet, and buckshot ripped into the wall above him. Creed threw his guns away from him, lying flat with both hands shielding his head as plaster sprayed down like snow to cover him.

'Just stay there, kid!' Anderson

recognized Huber's voice.

Above him, Jordan Hemphill towered like an avenging angel, aiming what looked like a Tranter pepper-box pistol at the lawman's head. Anderson started to turn, raising his pistols, knowing he was already far too late.

'Damn you, Anderson! You killed my boy!' The undertaker's face was a mask of pain and rage, tears furrowing the gaunt cheeks. Above the pistol, though, the eyes were cold, unpitying. 'Your turn to die!'

'Drop it, Pa!' Abigail shouted. She entered the room the same time as the shorter Huber, both of them toting shotguns from the saloon. Abigail levelled both barrels on the tall, black-clad figure as she called out, her blunt, freckled face angry and determined. 'You hear me, Pa? Drop the gun right now!'

Hemphill glanced once at his daughter, but made no move to lower the gun.

'You wouldn't shoot me, Abigail,' he

told her. 'Not your own father.'

Abigail choked and swallowed, tears filling her eyes as the shotgun wavered in her grasp. Hemphill had begun to smile, turning back to Anderson, when the other voice called out.

'Maybe not, but I would!' Dutchy Huber yelled. The thickset saloonman lined his weapon on Hemphill, eyeing the undertaker with a murderous expression. 'What's more, I got a whole barrel still to use, an' it's gonna be enough. Drop the goddamn gun!'

'May God forgive you all,' Jordan Hemphill said. He threw down the gun, moving to where Kedron crouched sobbing over the body of her brother. For a time he too stayed there, stroking the hair of his dead son as the tears ran down his face.

That's right, old man, Anderson thought. Now maybe you know how they felt in the Indian villages. He lowered the smoking pistols, feeling the sick weariness hit him the way it always did afterwards. Anderson clambered out of the coffin, and looked from Gilead and his folks to Abigail Hemphill. The tall, freckled woman had laid her shotgun down. Now she stood, wiping the tears that streamed from her eyes.

'Sure sorry, Abigail,' the dark man offered. 'Ain't no way I meant it . . . '

Abigail didn't answer, sparing him a wounded glance before she turned away. Anderson watched as she stood a couple of yards from the dead man and her father and sister, looking sadly down on all three. Eyeing that averted back, Anderson figured he didn't have a thing to say that was going to help her. And that hurt him worst of all.

Behind Huber and Abigail other men were shoving in through the doorway, storekeepers with rifles and shotguns in their hands. Now they grabbed Joey Creed, hauling him upright as he howled in pain.

'I cain't walk!' the kid yelled. 'Let go of me, goddammit! I'm tellin' you, my leg's busted!' He was still bawling as they dragged him outside.

'Doc kin take a look at him once he's in the jail-house,' Dutchy Huber said. He didn't sound too sympathetic. Scanning the bodies of Deacon and Gilead, and the three Hemphills, he switched his gaze back to Anderson. 'Good work, feller. You done us a favour, all right.'

'You reckon?' Anderson flexed his burned shoulder, grimaced as the bullet-crease reminded him. Across the room Kedron raised her beautiful head, fixing him scornfully with those huge soulful eyes.

'This is the worst day's work you have ever done, Mr Anderson,' she told him. 'God may forgive you. Be assured that I shall not.'

One of the townsmen caught her by the arm, and Kedron shook him off angrily, getting to her feet. Two others seized her sobbing father, pulling him away from Gilead's fallen body. Jordan Hemphill let them take him, shoulders slumped brokenly as they guided him out through the doorway. Kedron followed, not looking back.

'Should be a way better now at Kimball's Point,' Huber was saying. Reading the sombre expression of the tall man, he reached to lay a hand on Anderson's arm. 'Forget it, feller. You done what you had to. Come over my place, the drinks are on Dutch. What do you say?'

'Reckon I might just take you up on that, Dutchy,' Anderson said.

He shucked the dead shells from the pistols, stowed the guns in belt and holster. Anderson took a final look around the funeral parlour, where Deacon and Gilead lay among the coffins in a thinning haze of gunsmoke. The dark man breathed out slowly, and followed Huber for the door. He checked the girth that cinched the belly of the bay and nodded, satisfied. Anderson unhitched the horse from the rail, and took a grip on the saddle horn. He was all set to mount up when her voice broke silence behind him.

'So you're leaving, Mr Anderson,' Abigail said.

Hearing her, he turned quickly. She stood watching him from the doorway of Huber's saloon. From here, it was hard to read the expression on her face.

'That's right, Miss Abigail,' he told her.

Nothing to stay for now, he figured. A day ago they'd returned his saddle-bags, and the .45–70 carbine. Last week a telegram from Riggott had told how the outlaws who'd lived were being shipped back to the States to stand trial, and that the $1,500 reward on Magruder had been claimed. So Sharrock had his money, and wherever he was, chances were that Abe and the appaloosa were travelling with him.

Jordan Hemphill and Kedron were still in jail here, awaiting the county sheriff and the circuit judge. As the man behind the whole deal, the best Hemphill could hope for was a prison term. Maybe they'd go easier on Kedron. Then again, maybe they wouldn't.

'What happens to the totems?' Her question caught him by surprise, and he almost smiled.

'They'll go north, back to the Haidas. Canadian government will see they get 'em back.' Anderson thought about that a while, frowning. 'What they're gonna make of 'em, all chopped up that way, I can't rightly tell. It ain't gonna be the same as it was before, that's for sure. Maybe, with luck, Seal Caller's folks kin start again. I sure hope so.'

'At least they'll be where they ought to be,' Abigail said.

'Won't bring back the folks they lost neither, Abigail.'

'Nor my brother, Mr Anderson.' For a moment, her voice grew tight.

'Yeah. Guess not.' Anderson studied her warily, uncertain of what to tell her. 'Abigail, I want you to know that wasn't none of my doin'. I never aimed for him to die that way.'

'I know it.' From somewhere Abigail found a weary, washed-out smile. 'It was the outlaw, Creed, who killed him.

I'm sure you did your best to keep your word to me, Mr Anderson. Sadly, it was not to be.' She shrugged, as if shifting a huge weight from her shoulders. 'So what will you do now?'

'Head back to Mexico, ma'am,' Anderson told her. 'It's what they pay me for, I guess. How about you?'

'My father's funeral business will need to be run in his absence.' She eyed him levelly as she spoke. 'It seems only one of us is left to carry it on at present.'

Anderson met her gaze, not answering.

'It's a worthy calling, Mr Anderson,' Abigail said. 'That is, if it's run the way it should be. And that's how I intend to run it, you may be sure. Who knows, perhaps we shall regain our good name in time.'

'You'll be the best undertaker there ever was, Miss Abigail.'

She smiled at that, a faint flush touching the hard, freckled features.

'Perhaps.' Abigail stepped forward,

holding out her hand. 'In view of what has happened, friendship is scarcely appropriate, Mr Anderson. All the same, you have my respect. Allow me to wish you a safe journey home.'

'Thanks, Abigail.' Anderson shook her hand until it released its grip. 'Fact is, you saved my life, an' there ain't no way I aim to forget it. Here's hopin' things look up for you, an' thanks again.'

'Goodbye, Mr Anderson,' Abigail Hemphill said. She stood watching as he mounted up, and the bay gelding moved away from the rail.

'Give my best to Dutchy,' he told her, before he rode on.

She didn't answer, watching as man and horse loped down the empty street, and took the long road south.

We do hope that you have enjoyed reading this large print book.

Did you know that all of our titles are available for purchase?

We publish a wide range of high quality large print books including:
Romances, Mysteries, Classics
General Fiction
Non Fiction and Westerns

Special interest titles available in large print are:
The Little Oxford Dictionary
Music Book, Song Book
Hymn Book, Service Book

Also available from us courtesy of Oxford University Press:
Young Readers' Dictionary
(large print edition)
Young Readers' Thesaurus
(large print edition)

For further information or a free brochure, please contact us at:
Ulverscroft Large Print Books Ltd.,
The Green, Bradgate Road, Anstey,
Leicester, LE7 7FU, England.
Tel: (00 44) 0116 236 4325
Fax: (00 44) 0116 234 0205

The Valley of the Wolf was no place for strangers, but Chet Beautel was not the usual breed of drifter. He was a straight-shooting man of the mountains searching for something better than what lay behind. Instead, he encountered a new brand of terror enshrouded in a mystery which held a thousand people hostage — until he saddled up to challenge it with a mountain man's grit and courage, backed up by a blazing .45. If Wolf Valley was ever to be peaceful again, Chet Beautel would be that peacemaker.

RETURN TO RIO DIABLO

Wade Vanmarten

After killing the drug-crazed son of a powerful man, Deputy Sheriff Brimmer Stone is forced to resign his post and leave Houston. He and his best friend return to Rio Diablo, a wide-open Texas town that holds memories of youthful adventure and romance for them both. There, Stone rekindles a love affair, while his friend makes plans to take his new love away from the fancy house where she works and marry her. The sudden and brutal murder of his friend sends Stone on a quest for revenge that sets off a bloody war . . .

47 486